TEMPERANCE TOWN

TEMPERANCE TOWN

JOHN WILLIAMS

BLOOMSBURY

For Phil and Siân

First published 2004

Copyright © 2004 by John Williams

The moral right of the author has been asserted

Bloomsbury Publishing Plc, 38 Soho Square, London W1D 3HB

A CIP catalogue record for this book
is available from the British Library

ISBN 0 7475 7098 1

Typeset by Hewer Text Ltd, Edinburgh

All papers used by Bloomsbury Publishing are natural,
recyclable products made from wood grown in well-managed
forests. The manufacturing processes conform to the
environmental regulations of the country of origin.

Printed by Clays Ltd, St Ives plc

CONTENTS

AUTHOR'S NOTE

The Cardiff that appears in this book is an imaginary place that should not be confused with the actual city of the same name. Anyone who knows the city may be surprised to encounter assorted landmarks – the North Star, the Custom House, and so on – that no longer exist in Cardiff today. And being an imaginary city it goes without saying that the people who inhabit it are imaginary too.

MIKEY

A CHILD'S CHRISTMAS IN SPLOTT PART 1

Christmas was always a busy time of year for Mikey Thompson. He used to feel like Santa Claus. You know the way kids write out lists for Santa? Well, that's just what grown-ups would do for Mikey.

Take Linda, lived over the flats opposite. Nice girl, Mikey had a little thing with her, ten years ago easy. Having a bit of a hard time of it now though, what with the three kids and no job and no man putting nothing in the kitty since Karl was sent down Dartmoor. Anyway, this is how it worked: Mikey's in the Spar buying a few little bits and pieces and he bumps into Linda, right there by the chill cabinet full of Sunny Delight.

'Mikey,' she says, 'got a Christmas list for you. You want to pop over later on?'

'Sure,' says Mikey, and soon as Tina's busy watching *Jenny Jones*, Mikey's round there. Sits down on the settee, looks at the photos of her boys, has a cup of tea, and Linda shows him the list.

'Christ,' he says then, 'you're not planning on getting all this lot, are you?'

'No,' she says, 'well, depends what it costs, like,' and wriggles about a bit on her seat to make sure Mikey gets an eyeful, which is fine by Mikey. Though it doesn't mean any cut rate for Linda 'cause Mikey Thompson wasn't born yesterday.

'All right then,' says Mikey, 'you got a biro?' Linda passes him one and he goes through the list. First thing he does is put a mark by all the items too big for him to supply.

DVD player – why the hell did everyone want a DVD player this year, like a video that can't record. What's the point of that? – anyway no way he could manage one of them. Same with the microwave and the duvet.

Couple of things he wasn't sure about. Micro-scooter. Ordinarily he wouldn't touch anything in the bike range but these kids' scooters folded down to nothing, so he figured he'd have a go. Billy the Talking Bass he put a mark by. Even though it wasn't that big, he just couldn't face the piss-taking he'd get if he was caught with one of them.

What was left was all nice, easy stuff: jeans, lingerie, watch, perfume, three football shirts – two Man U, of course, and one Barcelona for the eldest lad.

'Any chance of getting the names on the back?' asked Linda. 'Two of them want Ryan Giggs and the other wants . . . Rivaldo, is it?'

Mikey shook his head. 'You want names, you just goes back in with the shirt and pays for it.'

'OK,' said Linda, then frowned. 'Did I put a mobile down on there?'

'No,' said Mikey. 'Anyway, can't get them.'

Mikey had a problem with mobiles. You need the box with the chip or whatever in and they never left those out on displays. No, the thing to do with mobiles was to nick them after they'd been bought. People were forever leaving their phones lying around on pub tables and stuff.

But Mikey didn't do that. He was a shoplifter pure and simple. He wasn't a pickpocket or a burglar, he didn't rob off regular people. Some people he knew, right, this time of year they're scouting the suburbs looking for Christmas parties going on. Then they're into the neighbours', nicking all the Christmas presents while they're drinking the mulled wine next door. But Mikey thought that was despicable. And you think that made him a hypocrite? Well, all Mikey could say was when you're a shoplifter you've got to take your dignity where you can find it.

He stood up, scanned the list and said, 'Anyway, s'already going to be a hundred quid easy, you want all that lot.'

'Hundred's all right, Mikey – that's what I was budgeting for.'

Budgeting? Mikey couldn't see how budgeting came into it, but you never knew. Maybe she'd hit the lottery for a few quid, more likely she was into Kenny for a ton, paying off at five per cent a month, just about clear it off by next Christmas. Still it wasn't Mikey's business to worry about where the money came from, he just had to make sure he got paid, and anyway he was saving her a fortune.

'Give us twenty for a deposit then, sweetheart,' he said, 'and I'll be round later on.'

'Any time,' said Linda with a bit of a wink and Mikey gave her a bit of a smile. No harm keeping your options open after all.

So Mikey's a man on commission now and he heads on into town. First place he goes in is KidzToyz and immediately he swings into action. Chatting away with the security guard on the door, oldish feller, complaining about the price of the toys, kids cost you a fortune these days, don't they, and so forth. And the security feller's nodding and laughing and saying, 'Don't quote me on this, but you want one of them scooters you're better off going to Splott Market,' and then Mikey's off into the store proper, objective already part-way achieved.

See, Mikey's tactic is the opposite of your regular shoplifter. Mikey goes for maximum visibility. Otherwise he'd have to try and be inconspicuous, and that wasn't really on, not in this country, knowing the way store detectives and that tend to feel about guys wandering round their shops and never buying anything.

Mikey walked the shelves of Pokemon stuff trying to remember if anyone had placed an order then shook his head. Funny that, couple of months ago all the kids were mad for the stuff – now it was about as fashionable as Pinky and Perky.

Never mind, looked like the only thing he needed in

the whole place really was the scooter. There was a whole pile of them right there in the middle of the store all boxed up and ready to go. Bollocks though, they really were pretty big. No way that was fitting inside your jacket, not even the oversized puffa Mikey was wearing. Go in a bag OK, mind, in fact Mikey was carrying one just the right size for it, but the security guy had seen him walk in with it practically empty, so it wouldn't take Sherlock Holmes to figure something might be going on if he came out with it full of scooter. And that was if he managed to load it in without the pissed-off-looking blonde he was pretty well convinced was a store detective noticing him. Oh well, maybe he'd come back later on.

Next stop the big store in the Hayes. Department stores were a favourite for Mikey, great rabbit warrens with lots of nice blind spots. Hell, you could even take the stuff in the lift. Lifts were great for checking whether any store detectives were taking an interest. Get in the lift, punch all the different floor buttons and you'll soon see if there's someone following you or not.

First up was menswear. Mikey did his usual routine of chatting up the girl on the till, none too subtly, waited till she got all embarrassed and started pretending to be busy phoning the accounts department or whatever and helped himself to a couple of Ben Shermans – one blue, one red as per Linda's instructions.

Then it was over to the lingerie. Lingerie was even easier. Men shopping for lingerie always looked dead nervous and uncomfortable and the sales staff had learned to deal with that by leaving them alone. And of course it crushed up nice and small. Quick routine with the lift then, just to make sure he wasn't being over-confident, but the coast was clear. Mikey positively sauntered back out on to the Hayes.

He peered in Waterstone's as he walked past. It was a crying shame no one ever seemed to order any books 'cause if ever there was a sitting target for shoplifters it was a bookshop. But the only time Mikey could re-member anyone asking him to steal them a book it was Billy Pinto asking him for something called *The Anarchist's Cookbook*, and like a fool Mikey had actually gone looking through the cookery sections for a week before someone told him what it was, basically a handbook for nutters who wanted to blow stuff up. Which when he thought about it sounded a lot more like Billy Pinto's kind of book than *The Naked Chef* or whatever.

Mikey carried on over to ABC Sports for the Man U tops. Now this was a tricky one. To say they were on the lookout for shoplifters in here was a total understate-ment. And no wonder either: forty quid for a footie top that changed about twice a season. You want to see a real daylight robbery then look no further.

Still, the second Mikey walked in there he could see he was in luck. Right ahead of him was a bunch of lads, fifteen, sixteen, probably ought to be in school but you couldn't imagine any of their teachers complaining that this lot weren't around. And they might as well have had signs attached to them saying we have come to make a completely pathetic attempt to nick a bunch of stuff. All

Mikey had to do was trail along behind them and watch them all troop into the changing room, oh so subtly trying on two shirts each and pretending they only had one.

Both the store detectives were staring after them practically salivating, so Mikey took the opportunity to slip two shirts down his trousers. Then as the boys walked out, loudly talking about what a rip-off the place was, Mikey lurked around near the exit, waited for the store detectives to be all over the lads and walked out. Sweet.

His shopping bag looking presentably full now. He headed back into KidzToyz on the way home, snaffled a scooter, casual as you like, and strolled on out, telling the feller on the door he was right, Splott Market got to be a better deal every time.

Took the whole lot round Linda's on his way back and she was well pleased. Wasn't too keen to part with the quids, of course, but then who was. Kept on hinting that they might be able to 'work something out'. But Mikey stayed firm, told her there were plenty of other people would happily pay good money for the gear, and she forked it over.

But then he hung around for a bit anyway, another cup of tea and so forth, and by the time he left it was pretty evident he had a standing invitation to pop down her chimney any time.

And that, with minor variations, was how things carried on for Mikey the whole fortnight coming up to Christmas. Mikey practically lost count of the number of shirts and CDs and bottles of perfume he'd lifted. Definitely felt like he was pushing his luck by Christmas Eve when he had the girl on the perfume counter in Howell's showing him half the stock while he kept on flirting till she just had to look away, and he flipped this hundred-pound bottle of Calvin Klein's Obsession – special order from Kenny Ibadulla for his missis, woe betide Mikey he didn't come back with that one – into his bag.

So it was a bit of a relief when he made it back home two o'clock on Christmas Eve afternoon without getting chased once by a store detective, let alone getting nicked.

Mikey Junior was there at the house all dressed up and excited waiting for Mikey to take him round to Black Caesar's for Kenny Ibadulla's annual kids' party.

Mikey was looking forward to it too. The sight of Kenny dressed up as Santa Claus never failed to make him laugh. There was Kenny – 364 days of the year the meanest bastard Mikey knew, Butetown's original gang-ster – looking like a big red pussycat, asking the children what they wants for Christmas and handing out the selection boxes. Never mind that half the mums there would be paying off Kenny for the presents for the next six months, you couldn't take it away from him, it was a nice gesture. And Mikey felt good too – least he was keeping the Christmas bills down for them.

By about six o'clock the party had started to become more of an adult affair. The kids were still there all running round, hyper as anything, but the DJ had switched from Steps to Garage and the bar had opened up, and Mikey was having a seasonal Malibu and trying it on with Maria like he did every Christmas, and who was to say this year wouldn't be the one she finally gave in, when it hit him. He'd done the Christmas shopping for half Butetown, he'd got a whole bunch of stuff stacked up under the tree for little Mikey, another micro-scooter, a robotic dog, WWF Smackdown 2 for the Playstation, everything he'd asked for. The one thing he didn't have was a present for Tina. She was going to bloody murder him he didn't get her something.

First off he tried to think if he had anything lying around he could give her, unwanted orders or whatever. Nice little set of undies from Ann Summers – girl he got them for said she didn't like the colour, so he'd been planning on giving them to Linda on Boxing Day – they'd be perfect, except no way was Tina ever going to fit into them.

Damn it, there had to be somewhere open. Sudden flash of inspiration: bound to be a big concert on in town, Stereophonics or Charlotte Church or whatever, pick her up a sweatshirt or something.

Double damn: no go again. He asked about a bit, nobody knew of anything like that going on in town. Think, think, think. What did Tina want?

Well, one thing for sure he wasn't going to find her a present standing here in Black Caesar's. His cousin Del was at the far end of the bar in no state to be going anywhere so Mikey borrowed his car keys and fetched Del's ancient Datsun, and drove straight into town. He couldn't believe it: six o'clock and everything was shut. Didn't they know this was the busiest time of year?

Whole centre of town there was nothing open apart from the bars and clubs which were all chock full of happy pissed-up young people who'd probably done their shopping weeks ago. Christ, there must be somewhere open. He decided to head over to the Bay Retail Park. Surely that would stay open late. Fat chance.

He was just motoring hopelessly though Grangetown on his way back home wondering what would piss off Tina the least, bottle of vodka from the Spar, or the too-small undies from Ann Summers, just give her a smile and pretend he thought she was that thin, or a carton of fags – there was an idea. Tina loved her fags. But, it had to be said, it wasn't exactly Christmassy, didn't really make it look like you'd been trying hard.

Then he saw it, a solitary lighted shop-front. He did a double take when he saw the name. The Feng Shui Superstore had to be as out of place as anything on Clare Road. But right now, it looked like a godsend. See, Mikey wasn't too sure what this feng shui business was, but Tina was forever chopsing on about it ever since she'd seen it on *Oprah* or *Richard and Judy* or something.

So Mikey goes in and the woman in there, who's giving it all the mystic East stuff, but Mikey's sure he went out with her sister once, asks him if he knows what he wants and he doesn't so she gives him the spiel about how you put the right things in the right places in your house and get good luck and wealth and happiness and all that. Which sounds about as plausible to Mikey as believing in Father Christmas.

But he doesn't say that, he just says well, what've you

got that's good for wealth then, and the woman shows him this, that and the other wind-chime and water feature, till finally he spots a carved Buddha at the back, the Buddha of the Infinite Beads or something, and she says yeah that'll definitely see you right and Mikey buys it – well, he figured his karma would never recover if he lifted it – and out he comes feeling as pleased as punch.

Next morning when little Mikey's already trying to play his video game while riding his scooter, Tina opens her present. He can see her about to go, 'What the fuck's this?' so he jumps in and says, 'It's feng shui, love, going to bring us wealth,' and she just changes, just like someone's flipped a switch, and instead of slagging him off gives him a big wet kiss, and just then little Mikey comes over and looks at the Buddha and says, 'Who's that, Father Christmas?' and then he looks at it a bit closer and says, 'Oh no, looks just like Dad.'

So Mikey and Tina look at the statue and both laugh 'cause it's true, it does look like Mikey, who's not as slim as he used to be, and then Tina looks at little Mikey, says, 'You got it right both times – that's your dad all right, he's a regular Santa Claus.'

'Oh c'mon, Mum,' says little Mikey then, 'how old d'you think I am? Everybody knows Santa's really your dad.'

THE RHONDDA RIVIERA

Kenny Ibadulla didn't like to deal with the retail side of his business. Too risky, plus you actually had to deal with the punters, which was depressing. But now and again though there was a situation where the top man needed to get involved personal.

That's what happened when one of Roger Hooper's people got in touch, wanting to place a very big order indeed. Now Kenny knew better than most that all kinds of people used cocaine these days but even so, Roger Hooper, Wales' very own financial-market multi-millionaire, wasn't your average punter.

So Kenny decided to manage this account himself. And it was going very well. First couple of times, Kenny just met with some kind of minion at Hooper's new resort and golf club over Bridgend way, by the outlet shopping mall. Third time he was there sitting in this executive suite at the resort – and a nice-looking place it was too, no question – in comes Roger Hooper himself, all casually dressed. Levis, polo shirt, and just so's you didn't forget he's rich, a great fuck-off Rolex on his wrist.

Kenny knew the signs from the off. Hooper was the kind of bloke liked to hang out with the odd outlaw, but Kenny let it go 'cause the feeling was mutual. So Hooper liked to mix with members of the criminal fraternity; well, Kenny like to mix with currency-speculating millionaires. 'Cause one thing Kenny knew, if he was ever going to make some serious money, he had to get out of dealing and into the stock exchange – the places the real money got made.

So they meet a few times and then, just casual like, Roger says, 'How about a game of golf then?'

'Sure,' says Kenny, who's been looking out at the golf course Roger's built there and thinking it really does look the business. So here's his invitation to mix with the big boys.

It was only during the ride back to Butetown that Kenny remembered one little problem – he didn't play golf. Didn't bother Kenny too much, he'd always been good at sports. Not just rugby, though everyone knew Kenny Ibadulla had been a hell of prospect when he was younger. He was a fearsome baseball player in the summer and his snooker wasn't bad either. So Kenny couldn't see a big problem in principle. It was just that if he was going to play golf with bloody Roger Hooper he'd better get familiar with the basics beforehand.

First thing he needed was someone to caddy for him. That took a bit of thinking 'cause most of the boys Kenny had working with him weren't the kind of fellers you wanted hanging around the Rhondda Riviera Resort. In fact it was only when he popped into the bookies looking for Col and found Mikey Thompson in there chatting up the cashier that Kenny realised he'd found his man. Mikey looked like a caddie for starters, sawn off as he was, and he had the gift of the gab all right, could fit in anywhere, Mikey could.

So he asks Mikey if he'd like to earn fifty quid for an afternoon's work and Mikey goes yeah sure, Kenny, who d'you want me to kill, and Kenny laughs like you do with Mikey and says no, bra, we're going to play some golf, and it's Mikey's turn to laugh, thinking Kenny's joking.

But Kenny's not, of course, and half an hour later the two of them are in the big American Golf shop out in Ely – which always made Kenny laugh. You got two shops in the whole of Ely more or less. One of them sells mobiles – of course – and the other's a golf shop. Anyway they get in there and it's a different world all of a sudden.

'Can I help you, sir?' says the manager bloke, looking nervous like people mostly did when they saw Kenny.

'Yeah,' says Kenny. 'I wants to play some golf,' and the bloke practically sighs with relief.

'Come to the right place, sir,' says the bloke. 'Well, let's start with the clubs.'

And so the bloke points Kenny towards a wall lined with golf clubs and wonders how much sir would like to spend. Kenny doesn't have a clue but then his eyes fall on a set of Wilsons marked down from £500 to half-price and says how about those, and the bloke says good choice sir and leads Kenny to the back of the store where there's a miniature driving range set up and he hands Kenny a club and Kenny just lashes at a ball with such ferocity that the bloke can't help stepping backwards.

'Yeah,' says Kenny, 'these'll do fine. Now, what else do I need?'

'Shoes, sir,' says the bloke and Kenny follows him over to look at a display of the worst-looking footwear Kenny has ever seen in his life. Most of it is in brown and cream with these stupid frilly flaps going over the front of the shoe. Eventually though the bloke digs out a plain black pair that aren't too horrible and Kenny takes them, then wanders over to look at the clothes.

There were still plenty of vile Nick Faldo sweaters, but thankfully, since Tiger Woods had come into the game, Nike had knocked up some decent-looking gear. There wasn't a lot in Kenny's Xtra-giant size of course but eventually he got a nice black-and-white polo top and a pair of black trousers. The whole outfit should look pretty damn mean, he thought: even the golf bag was black.

Mikey helped carry the gear out to the jeep, the manager bloke grovelling after them after Kenny'd paid him off from a serious wad of fifties.

'Right, boss,' said Mikey then, 'where to now?'

Kenny shrugged. 'I dunno, Mikey. You know any golf courses?'

Mikey frowned for a moment then smiled. 'Yeah, Ken,' he said. 'I knows just the place.'

Ten minutes later Kenny was steering the jeep north out of Cardiff then through Tongwynlais and up past Castell Coch into some proper countryside, Mikey telling Kenny about this girl from Whitchurch he'd been knocking off, liked to come up here in her car with Mikey to get a little privacy from her husband. Then there they were, right up on top of the Caerphilly Mountain, pulling into something called the Castell Heights Golf Club.

For the next three hours, Kenny worked on his swing. First hole took him thirty-five shots to get down, and Mikey frankly feared for his life when he saw the face on Kenny after missing his twelfth putt. But gradually, through sheer force of will, Kenny started to get on top of the game. He finished the ninth hole with a par and was so chuffed he gave Mikey a full ton instead of the fifty they'd agreed.

'All right, Mikey,' he said. 'Pick you up eleven o'clock Friday. We're going to the Rhondda Riviera.'

Standing at the first tee, in front of the clubhouse, which was designed as a scale model of the Parthenon, Roger Hooper introduced Kenny to the other two blokes were going to be making up the foursome.

'Did I tell you I was going into the film business, Kenny?' he said.

'No,' said Kenny, momentarily distracted by the sunlight catching Hooper's Rolex.

'Yes indeed, we're just starting work on our first film, an action adventure. You'll never guess what it's about.'

'Search me,' said Kenny, a little more animated now. He'd always had a bit of a fantasy about getting into the film business and here he was about to play golf with the kind of fellers actually made films. This was the kind of life he could get used to, instead of having to deal with two-bit drug dealers fancied themselves as Yardies even though they came from Llanrumney.

'Well,' said Hooper, 'it's about this successful business-man who leads a double life as a kind of super crime-stopper, battling against drug lords and gang leaders, you know, cleaning up the city for decent people.'

'Uh, huh,' said Kenny, trying not to laugh.

'Yes indeed,' said Hooper, 'and these two gentlemen here are the producers who are going to bring my vision to the big screen, Jason Lowndes and Simon Disolo. Jase, Simes, meet Kenny Ibadulla' – Hooper made a flourish with his hands – 'South Wales' leading drug baron.'

Kenny couldn't believe it. The world he moved in people didn't go round announcing other people's business like that.

'Businessman, Roger,' he said. 'I'm a businessman.'

Roger winked at Jason and Simon. 'Of course you are, Kenny, of course you are.'

Kenny was not in a good mood. He was standing in a bunker by the eighth green waiting for Mikey to pass him the sand wedge and you could see the veins standing out on his neck.

'Easy, boss,' said Mikey. 'Don't let those tossers get to you.'

When Hooper's mates weren't talking to Kenny in what they imagined street slang to be, they were mouthing off about the movie business, kept going on about just being back 'from the Coast'. Oh yeah, says Mikey, Pembrokeshire? No, says one of the guys, the feller called Simon, LA. Yeah, says Mikey, pleased to hear that, didn't think they made a lot of movies in Pembrokeshire, and the two guys looked at each other not sure if Mikey was a halfwit or winding them up.

Kenny wouldn't have minded them so much if they weren't beating him. One thing Kenny hated was losing at any sporting activity whatsoever. Plus, in Kenny's line of business, his physical presence was a big part of how he got people to fall in line. And now here he was losing to the kind of snotty weaklings he could normally have scared the shit out of.

No, Kenny was not a happy man as he stared down at the ball lying obstinately in the middle of the sand trap. He raised his wedge behind him then brought it down in a furious swing that created a fair-sized sand blizzard in the bunker and moved the ball itself a grand total of eighteen inches.

Kenny just stood there, practically hyperventilating, Mikey standing back, well out of club-swinging range. Then there's a shout of 'Fore' and another ball appears out of nowhere and lands in the bunker. A moment later the feller called Simon appears.

'Oh,' says Simon, 'You here too? Hard luck, mate.'

Then Simon jumps down into the sand trap and has a look. His ball was in a significantly worse lie than Kenny's, right by the lip of the bunker.

'Tell you what, sport,' he says after a moment. 'Fancy a little side wager – which one of us gets closer to the pin?'

'All right,' says Kenny, determined not to be faced down by this geek. 'What d'you have in mind?'

Simon shrugs. 'Oh nothing much, a oncer, say'. Then he pauses and taps the side of his nose, 'Or a gram of your finest, if that's easier.'

Kenny just stares at the bloke incredulously. Did this guy really think he, Kenny Ibadulla, walked round the place with a load of little wraps of coke looking to get busted like a twat? What kind of lightweight did they take him for?

'No,' he said, 'a ton will be fine.'

Kenny's ball was a little further away so he went first. Once again he just gave it everything, sand everywhere again, but this time the ball lifted off the ground and – hallelujah – bounced on to the green no more than three yards from the pin, heading straight for it.

'Nice one, boss,' said Mikey, as the ball looked certain to drop, but then it picked up speed, rolled on for a good six feet beyond the pin. Still, it was about as good a result as Kenny could have hoped for.

'Nice shot, sir,' said the bloke Simon, and made a show of indecision before taking his sand wedge and effortlessly chipping the ball out of the bunker and on to the green, ending up no more than a foot away from the pin.

Kenny handed over the hundred without a word. Same thing happened on the next hole more or less, except it was whose putt would go closest this time and it was Jason, not Simon, who made the bet. Result was the same though. Kenny left looking like a dick handing over another ton. Same tap of the nose from Jason as well and suggestion that payment in kind would be quite acceptable, nudge, nudge.

Finally, there they were at the eighteenth tee and this time it's Roger Hooper himself comes out with the final bet.

'Tell you what, chaps,' he says, 'little wager on who can hit the longest drive. Course with a feller the size of Kenny here the rest of us don't have much of a chance, but still . . . What d'you say, guys – a grand each, winner takes all?'

Jason and Simon, the two film-making muppets, nodded and smiled. All three of them turned to Kenny.

'All right with you, bro?' said Jason.

Kenny bit back the urge to break Jason's neck for calling him bro, just smiled and said, 'I dunno . . . a grand . . . you fellers wouldn't mind taking it in kind, would you?' and tapped the side of his nose.

The three stooges smiled broader than ever. 'No, indeed that'd be fine,' said Hooper.

They drew lots for who went first. Simon was first off, Kenny third and Hooper last.

Simon's drive sailed way up into the air and Roger Hooper – another man who didn't like to lose – sucked in his breath as it seemed to go on and on, but then it bounced and seemed to kick off to the left and headed relentlessly toward the rough to the side of the fairway.

'Hard luck, man,' said Hooper. 'Try and keep it on the fairway next time.'

Simon grimaced, doing his best to look like it meant nothing to him.

Jason went next and Kenny could see what had happened to Simon's ball preying on his mind. Jason hit the ball with something less than his usual power, concentrating on keeping it on the fairway, and so the ball went dead straight but nowhere near as far as Simon's ball had gone.

Hooper got some kind of electronic gizmo out of his pocket and aimed it at the ball.

'A hundred and ninety yards, Jase,' he said, 'give or take. Not going to scare Kenny here much that, is it?'

Kenny swallowed, nervous as he could remember being. Mikey handed him a wood and Kenny walked up to the ball, addressed it quickly, then took the most almighty swing at it. If he'd missed the ball he'd probably have torn every muscle above the waist. But he didn't miss, he hit the ball fair and square and it shot down the fairway, just as far as Simon's ball had gone. Kenny held his breath as it bounced, but unlike Simon's ball the bounce was true. The ball carried on for another fifty yards or so before coming to a halt, just to the left of centre of the fairway.

Hooper raised his eyebrows then operated his gizmo again.

'Two hundred and fifty yards, Kenny,' he said. 'Looks like the pot's yours.'

Hooper's casualness was belied though by the amount of time he spent choosing a club. Eventually he brought out one Kenny hadn't seen before, a wood with a titanium shaft.

'Jesus, Roger,' said Simon when he saw it, 'thought only Tiger himself had one of those.'

'Hmm,' said Hooper. 'Actually, Earl – Tiger's dad, you know – gave it to me himself when we were playing in Valderrama.'

That shut Simon up all right and made Kenny pause for thought too.

And sure enough Roger Hooper walked up to his ball, casual as you like, swung, and the ball just seemed to go for miles. On and on it went, didn't bounce for the first time till it was past Jason's ball and comfortably overtook Kenny's ball before finally coming to rest.

'Two hundred and seventy-five,' said Hooper, consulting the gizmo. 'A new course record, I think. Now, chaps, time to pay up.'

Jason pulled out a cheque book and wrote out a cheque. Simon counted off from a roll of fifties.

Roger Hooper turned to Kenny.

'You said you'd like to pay in kind, so what shall we say – ten grams OK?'

Kenny raised his eyebrows. 'I can do better than that for you, Rog,' he said. 'Make it twenty.'

'You're too kind,' said Hooper.

'No worries,' said Kenny. 'Mikey, pass me a ball, you know, one of the special ones.'

Mikey looked at Kenny quizzically for a moment then dug into the bag, brought out a brand-new Titleist.

Kenny took it, made a show of examining it carefully then handed it to Roger.

'There you go,' he said. 'Twenty grams safely packed inside. Little idea I got after visiting your place last time, Rog.'

'Nice one, bro,' said Roger, taking the ball.

Driving back to Butetown in the Jeep, Mikey turned to Kenny.

'Didn't tell me you were packing your gear into golf balls, Ken.'

Kenny turned his head from the road for a moment and stared at Mikey.

'Mikey, sometimes I wonder about you.' He paused for a moment then carried on. 'You got any idea what they put in the middle of golf balls?'

Mikey shook his head, a smile spreading across his face.

'Me neither, Mikey boy, me neither. But I sure as hell wouldn't like to snort any of it.'

Back in the Rhondda Riviera clubhouse, sat round a table in the VIP lounge, Roger, Jason and Simon came to much the same conclusion.

CASANOVA MIKEY

Mikey was watching too much TV. He blamed the digital TV people. There'd been a bit of a screw-up on their computer and he was getting the whole package for free. Well, free apart from the little tip to his cousin Sean, who might have added a little helping hand to the computer screw-up.

Anyway, one way or another, there was Mikey with no money and two hundred TV channels to watch, even if half of them were showing Destiny's Child videos at any given moment. What better way to keep a feller out of trouble? That's what he kept telling Tina every time she'd get a bit aereated with him lying on the couch, middle of the day, switching between ancient episodes of *EastEnders* and the Channel Four racing. 'You rather I was out there hustling?' he'd say. 'You're always on about how I can't be trusted out of your sight, well, here I am right where you can see me.'

Course Tina never appreciated the sacrifice he was making, giving up the chance to hang out down on

Mermaid Quay, looking for any Swedish tourists wanted to take a guided tour round the real Tiger Bay, in favour of lying on his couch watching Homer Simpson lying on his couch. Longer life went on, the more, Mikey felt, he had in common with that feller, except for the hair.

Still, at heart, Mikey was a go-getter and, even when watching TV, he couldn't help but be scheming. Way he saw it, he was an ideas man. That's why he'd never been too successful in the crime business where ideas were all very well but being big and violent was even better. But in the world of TV – this is what Mikey was figuring out – it was all about ideas. Take that *Who Wants to be a Millionaire?* Bloke thought that up made a bloody fortune. Same with all these shows that were on now, these reality things – *Big Brother*, *Survivor*, all of them – it was just a question of coming up with the right idea.

'How about this one Col' – Col had dragged him out for a little drink and game of pool down the Ship – 'you take these six people, yeah, like on *Big Brother*, and you get them all living in this house together.'

'Like on *Big Brother*,' chips in Col.

'Yeah, yeah, like on *Big Brother*, but here's the difference, right – you know how on *Big Brother* they never shag each other, right?'

'Right,' says Col, already shaking his head.

'Right, well, in this version the whole point is they all have to shag each other.'

'What, the blokes have to shag each other?'

'No,' says Mikey, getting exasperated, 'just the ones of

the opposite sex or whatever, right. And then they vote off the one who's the worst shag.'

'What happens if there's just two blokes left at the end though?'

Mikey thought about it, screwed his face up. 'Bollocks.'

He scratched his head. 'All right, all right, I got another one. You know that *Survivor* thing, right, where they stick them on a desert island and they got to survive. Well, instead of the island, right, what you do is you take some, like, straight people and you dump them here . . .'

'What, this pub? It ain't that bad, Mikey.'

'Nah, just round here in general, like – the docks, right – and how it works is they've got no money and they got to survive, they got to learn how to hustle – that's what I'd call it, *Hustler* – and like you'd call in the experts, teach them how to do stuff – dealing, lifting, pimping, fraud, whatever. Last one standing – doesn't get nicked and makes some money – they're the winner.'

'Oh yeah, and who would these experts be?'

'That's the thing, Col, fellers like you and me.'

'Sweet,' says Col, 'yeah, I can just see myself watching that. From bastard jail.'

'C'mon, bra, it's for TV. Police can't arrest you, you're on TV.'

'Yeah, right, Mikey,' said Col, shaking his head and laughing. 'But seriously, talking of hustling business, you know what I've been worrying about?'

Mikey shrugged, pissed off that Col wouldn't take his ideas seriously. Col carried on anyway.

'What I'm worrying about is this legalise cannabis business.'

'How d'you mean? Got to be good for business, innit?'

Col shook his head. 'Nah, man, it goes legal they'll cut out the little man, I'm telling you. You be buying it in Tesco Extra or your newsagent. Packets of them, all made up by Marlboro. You know what they're going to call them?'

'What?'

'Marley. Marley cigarettes.'

Mikey started to laugh but Col shushed him.

'True fact, man. They copyrighted the name – Marley cigarettes – you believe that? Bob'd be rolling in his grave.'

Mikey thought about it. 'Still, they got to get the stuff from somewhere.'

'Yeah, they'll be growing big plantations of the stuff out in Jamaica.' He shook his head. 'Bad news for the little guy, I'm telling you.'

'No, Col, you got the expertise, you got to be like a specialist producer, tell them your stuff's free range, organic or whatever.'

Col smiled. 'You know what, Mikey boy, that was actually halfway intelligent.'

'Yeah, well,' said Mikey, still pissed off that Col wouldn't take his TV ideas seriously.

By the time he'd got home, he was determined he'd show Col. How hard could it be really to come up with a decent idea? This was a world where filming some old bat from up the Valleys failing her driving test again and again counted as a good idea.

Plus, Mikey had a contact in the media. Girl named Kim worked at the BBC. She had made this documentary about drug dealing in the docks a while back. Mikey had been her research assistant, like. Which meant that when, surprise, surprise, she hadn't been able to find any real drug dealers wanted to go on the telly, he'd helped her fake the whole thing up. He'd helped her out in one or two other ways, and all. Yeah, Kim was just the person. All he needed was the idea.

He was awake half the night trying to come up with something, listening to Tina snoring lightly next to him, thinking driving school, cruise liner, hospital – what hadn't been done? Maybe a solicitor's office – Lord knows, you sat round Mikey's brief's office for the afternoon you'd hear some unbelievable tales but, nah, the legal problems'd be terrible.

Then again that trading-places show was pretty good – where they get like this classical musician to be a rave DJ or whatever – Mikey quite fancied that. They could take Mikey and make him some stock-exchange feller – except that wasn't really a new idea and he was getting off the point: this needed to be like a game show sort of thing.

Finally, around four in the morning, he got it. Well, he got something worth a try.

So, ten in the morning, right after taking little Mikey to school, he was on the phone to the BBC. Got through to Kim straight away.

31

Sounded a bit flustered at first, like she'd just got into work that second, and took her a moment or two to remember who Mikey was, which pissed him off a bit and even when she did it wasn't like, 'Whoa, Mikey, that was the best night of my life,' but more like, 'Oh yeah, Mikey, it's not about that documentary, is it?' like he was going to blackmail her or something, tell her bosses how that Yardie drug supremo they filmed undercover was actually Mikey's cousin Del from Ely.

But anyway she sounds all relieved when Mikey says, 'No, none of that. Actually I've got an idea for a show.'

'Oh right,' says Kim, 'great.' Then there's a second where she obviously realises she doesn't want to sound too enthusiastic about some geezer from the docks suggesting an idea. 'Well,' she carries on, 'why don't you email it over and I'll have a look at it – not sure how soon, right up to my eyes at the moment, but I'm sure I'll . . .'

Email! No way is Mikey going to email over an idea as hot as this, risk it getting nicked by any passing secretary. Plus, to be honest, it's only little Mikey who has any idea how to operate the computer and he's in primary school at the minute.

'Look,' he says, 'I'd sooner meet in person, like, if that's all right.'

There's a pause at the other end.

'Well,' she says eventually, 'normally I like to see something in writing but seeing as it's you, Mikey, I'm sure I could manage a quick chat if you can come up here, say about twelve-thirty?'

'See you there,' says Mikey and puts the phone down. Sweet.

Took a little while to persuade Col to lend him his clapped-out Audi. Col finally gave in when he heard where Mikey was going, saying he could make a couple of little deliveries while he was up there.

Twelve-thirty on the dot – which was something of an all-time record, anyone who knew Mikey could tell you – there he was talking to the feller on reception at the BBC, who gave him a bit of a knowing look when he says he's come to see Kim, like she's a bit of a goer, that one, isn't she?

And she was. Looking better than ever as she comes out of the lift wearing a nice little summer dress, hair still hennaed, but grown out a bit since last time, more of a softer feminine look. Fine by Mikey.

'All right, girl?' he says, lets her kiss him on both cheeks, like hey, we're in the media now, and follows her into the canteen.

Kim gets a salad and Mikey goes for the full shepherd's pie, all the works, might as well make sure he gets something out of the meeting, and then they sit down by the window and he starts his pitch.

'All right, girl,' he says, 'this is how it goes. You get four blokes, right, all smart-looking geezers, and they've got all day to see how many girls they can get to meet them in the pub at eight o'clock that night.'

Kim looks at him, a bit quizzical. 'Sort of like *Street-mate*?'

'Yeah,' says Mikey, 'but competitive. Also I was thinking you could have like a side-bet thing, like a special prize for who can pull the ugliest bird.'

Kim rolled her eyes. 'Oh c'mon, Mikey, that's horrible, that's sadistic.'

Mikey shrugged. 'Thought that was the whole point of these programmes.'

'Up to a point,' says Kim, 'but that's just sexist.'

'All right, fair enough,' says Mikey, putting his hands up. 'OK, that's going too far, but the basic idea, yeah, you like that?'

Kim sat back, smiled at Mikey. 'Well, it's not exactly BBC material, is it?'

Mikey frowned. He hadn't thought about that. Two hundred channels on your TV, you forget which one you're watching. 'No good then?'

'Oh no,' said Kim, 'I wouldn't say that. I've been doing a little bit of moonlighting for one or two independent companies – might be interested in something like this. It's definitely got potential. Have you thought about the details though, how it would work?'

Mikey took a moment to answer. Detail wasn't really his thing. 'I was thinking,' he improvised, 'each of the guys would have like a hidden camera attached to them to record all their chat-up lines and stuff.'

Kim nodded. 'Yeah, no problem. How about location?'

Mikey shrugged. 'I figured each guy could choose their own location, like one guy might want to work in town, another guy might prefer to try the park, then again, you take me, for instance, I take more of a freestyle approach.'

Kim's eyebrows went up. 'Oh, you think you could be one of the contestants?'

Mikey smiled. She was definitely going for it. The old Mikey charm clearly worked with this one — shame he couldn't remember more about the little thing they'd had together, obviously made more of an impression on her. 'Sure, I *could* do it. I wasn't *thinking* of doing it myself but . . . yeah, sure.'

Kim's smile broadened. 'Great,' she said. 'I tell you what, why don't we give the idea a try-out right away? You up for that?'

'Sure,' says Mikey, 'but how d'you mean?'

'I don't know, I was thinking maybe I'd get you a hidden camera and you could — how did you put it? — try a bit of freestyling around the building.'

'You sure?' says Mikey, thinking, Christ, he'd heard things took for ever to get developed on TV — this was coming along at warp speed. Well, best not lose the momentum and, hey, when had Mikey Thompson ever turned down the opportunity to spend an afternoon persuading women to go out with him?

'All right,' he said, 'let's go for it.'

So, twenty minutes later Kim has him all fitted up with a little hidden camera fixed into his sports bag, just on top of Col's merchandise, and he's leaning on her assistant's desk, nice little blonde piece fresh out of college, and he's giving her some lyrics.

It's all corny old stuff – you got such lovely eyes, all that stuff. Eyes are always good, practically everyone thinks they've got nice eyes. You tell a girl she's got a nice bum, she'll either smack you one or spend half an hour going on about how it's too big – like that was ever a problem in Mikey's book. Anyway, Mikey was a firm believer that the corny old stuff was still what worked at the end of the day – no one gets too much flattery.

Ten minutes' work and she hasn't quite agreed to meet but he's got her mobile number and soon as he's out of the office he sends her a bit of a saucy text message, which he reckons ought to tip her over the edge.

Then he heads back downstairs to the canteen where he'd noticed a nice-looking girl cleaning up the tables and she's another definite maybe by the time he's finished there.

Then it's back into the lift where some uptight cow tells him to eff off before he's hardly started, but he's forgotten about that soon enough 'cause he's just walking down this corridor looking a bit lost when this girl calls out, 'Mikey!' and it's this piece was like a runner or whatever on the documentary Kim made before and she's dead keen, yeah, sure, she's meeting some friends up town later on, why doesn't Mikey come on down? Result.

One definite, two maybes. Surely that should be enough to show Kim. So he heads back upstairs to Kim's office, has another little tilt at the assistant but maybe he overdid it a bit with the text message 'cause she's a bit standoffish now but what the hell, and then he's into

Kim's office, handing over the camera and saying have a look at that lot darlin', I'm telling you, it's a winner, this series, a winner all the way, girl.

So Mikey headed home feeling well chuffed. Starts telling everyone how he's going to have his own TV show and they're all going like, 'Yeah, Mikey, sure, we believe you,' but Mikey's calm, it's clearly in the bag.

After three or four days without a phone call though he wasn't so sure. Even less sure when he starts trying to phone Kim and can't get past the assistant.

Another fortnight and, well, Mikey's had enough of people going, 'Oh when's your TV show then, Mikey.' In fact he's about ready to go back on the ships, people don't stop chopsing on about it, when he gets a call from some woman from some TV production company he's never heard of, saying she wants to bike round an advance cassette of his programme.

Now this had him a bit puzzled. How could they be sending him a tape of his programme? They hadn't even agreed to make it yet. He phoned Kim again, she still wouldn't speak to him, but just then the courier showed up with the tape and Mikey stuck it in the video and after about ten seconds he could see why Kim hadn't been answering his phone calls.

The giveaway came with the title – *Britain's Crummiest Casanovas* – which came up over pictures of four different blokes, three of whom looked like complete tossers and the other one was Mikey himself. Next it cut to the studio where some smug fat bird was getting what sounded like an audience of hen-night party-goers worked up with promises that they were about to see the saddest chat-up lines left in captivity.

Well, Mikey just sat there in shock as the programme played out. Kim had done him up like a kipper. The camera he'd had in his bag – and now, come to think of it, he was wondering if it really had been a camera at all – well, it certainly wasn't the only hidden camera about the place. 'Cause there was Mikey, lecherous as life, walking into this office sitting down next to this girl and spieling all these chat-up lines that had the audience in hysterics. Christ, how was he ever going to live this down? Double Christ, he knew the answer to that – he wouldn't have to live it down – the second Tina saw the show he'd be a dead man.

Mikey had to go for a walk just to get over the shock, the betrayal of it. What a total bitch. How dare she? He phoned up the number on the back of the tape, asked if Kim was there and, much to his surprise, got put through right away.

'Like the show, Mikey?' she says, bright as a button. Christ, he felt like smacking her.

'I'll bloody sue you,' he said, sounding pathetic even to himself.

'No you won't, you signed a release.'

'No, I didn't.'

'Yes, you did.'

Mikey thought about it. He remembered signing something, an expenses form for his lunch, she'd said. Bitch, bitch, bitch.

'Why?' he said finally.

'Why?' said Kim laughing. 'Why? Should have thought of why when you didn't bother bloody phoning me after we'd done the nasty, shouldn't you?'

Mikey shook his head. A woman scorned, or what. What was her problem with seeing a bit of a laugh for what it was. Just a bit of a celebration after they'd pulled off a scam together. Scam? Wait a minute, Mikey thought. Maybe there was a way out of this.

'So when's the programme going out?' he asks.

'Next Tuesday, Sky digital,' says Kim. 'Enjoy,' and she's about to put the phone down when Mikey says, 'Wait.'

And she hesitates and Mikey jumps in with, 'Course, I suppose your boss knows about those fake drug dealers we set up in the documentary before?'

There was a sharp intake of breath at the other end of the line.

'You total bastard,' she said eventually.

Mikey punched his fist in the air. He'd got her.

And so next Tuesday there's Mikey and Tina watching TV as per usual and on comes this *Crummiest Casanovas* show and funnily enough there's only three lucky victims on and Tina's laughing along and Mikey turns to her and says you just wonder what sort of mind thinks this kind of rubbish up.

TIGER PRINCESS

Mikey had always quite fancied management. Any fool could see it was where the money was. You look at them, S Club 7, Steps, all that shit, you could be damn sure it was the manager making the money, not the girls, bunch of game-show hostess types in bra tops. He'd been thinking about it for a while, the way you do watching TV. It's Saturday night, you've not enough money in your pocket to go out, and you're stuck inside watching bastard Jim Davidson, you got to be looking for an angle.

And how hard could it be? Find a bunch of fit-looking girls can sing a bit, get one of the boys to write a few songs for them – how could you go wrong? Nothing too tacky, of course, none of that teenybopper crap, something a bit classier, like Destiny's Child, say. Mikey liked them. Nice-looking girls too, which helped, of course, even if you could see a mile off the kind of stuck-up church-choir types they were. It might not exactly impress the boys to say you'd been listening to the new Destiny's Child but fair play to them he'd heard the new one on Nickelodeon the other day – watching with little Mikey, you know – and it wasn't bad. Yeah, something like that would be OK.

As for the management side of things, Mikey figured it couldn't be too different from what a few of the blokes he knew did, looking after some girl makes a living using her assets. He'd never got on too well in the pimping game himself, but he simply put that down to being too much of a decent bloke, too damn soft and, to be honest, none too keen on getting in a fight. Way he saw it, in the pop business chances were your girls didn't pull a knife on you too often.

Only question really was where to start. School would be good, he thought, get a bunch of sixteen-year-olds, lot of enthusiasm, not too clever with contracts. Come to think of which, he'd better have a word with his brief, see if he could sort him out with some kind of standard contract – as used by sharks everywhere, that kind of thing. Schoolgirls ought to be less chopsy too, with a bit of luck. Only problem, it was a right pain in the arse getting all the way over to the school. He'd popped round, asked Col if he'd mind driving him over Fitzalan and Col had given him a bit of a look. 'Jumping the cradle, are we now?' he'd said, so what with one thing and another it took him a couple of days to get it together.

Course, minute he got there he could see it was a bad idea. God knows what he was expecting to find. A bunch of girls standing on the corner by the sweet shop singing harmonies together? Well, surprise, surprise, it didn't quite work out like that.

First thing happened was he walked straight into a girl named Donna who he'd had a little thing with long, long time ago. She's standing by the gate waiting for her eleven-year-old to come out take him to his karate lesson. And so he's stuck there talking to this Donna, who, frankly, the years have not been kind to, looking scrawny as fuck and still got the loudest voice he'd ever heard – which is saying something in Cardiff where half the women seem to be in perpetual bloody foghorn practice.

Eventually, thank Christ, her little boy comes out, a mouthy little bastard in a Man U top, and Donna pisses off, but by then it looks like Mikey's blown it. Started to feel like just another dad come to take his kids home, not a top-flight music-biz entrepreneur looking for new talent.

Still, fair play to Mikey, he gave it a go anyway. Saw a bunch of fine-looking sixth-form girls come out together, all lighting up at once second they got to the school gates. He went up to the one in the middle, tall girl with braids.

'You ever done any singing, sweethearts?' he asked.

'Why, you fucking dance?' she said, and her mates all laughed like this was the funniest thing they'd ever heard.

'Look,' he said, 'I'm serious. I'm looking for some girls to join a group. Kind of Destiny's Child type thing and I saw you beautiful young ladies together, and I reckoned you've got the looks for it.'

That stopped them for a moment. One thing with girls, you could never overestimate their vanity. Flattery had always been a key weapon in Mikey's armoury. Lot of blokes couldn't do it, all that corny bullshit, your eyes are so beautiful, blah, blah, thought it was too stupid, but that was Mikey's strength. Nothing was beneath him, not if it worked.

'Oh yeah,' said another of the girls, little Asian-looking piece. 'And who are you then?'

'Me,' said Mikey, 'I'm . . . oh I been around the music business for years, kind of a freelance talent scout and manager at the moment. Lot of contacts. It's all about who you knows, see, in this business. You knows the Sugababes, yeah?'

The girls nodded.

'Well,' lied Mikey, 'it was me who discovered them.'

'No, it wasn't,' said the tall girl. 'I seen it on the telly, it was this lady, she's their manager.'

'Yeah, yeah, course,' said Mikey. 'Lovely lady too, but she didn't do it all by herself, you know. That's just the way they put it out to the press like. No she, um, the girls' manager, right, she had to have someone see her girls, spot the talent and take them to the right record company and stuff.' Mikey pointed to his chest. 'Mikey Thompson's the man.'

There was a pause.

'Mikey Thompson,' said another girl, light-skinned with freckles, 'I knows who you are. You knows my dad, innit. He never said you was in the music business.'

Bollocks. Mikey placed her now – Carlton's little girl, Shelley or something. Time to move things along.

'Anyway,' he said, 'question is, you girls sing or not?'

Then, before any of them could answer he carried on, 'Silly question. Course you can. Tell you what, how about you come and audition for me tonight. Nine o' clock in the community centre.'

The girls looked at each other. Mikey could see vanity battling it out with cynicism. He relaxed, only one winner in that situation. The girls went into a little huddle, whispered furiously, then the freckled girl, Shelley or whatever, turned to Mikey and said, 'Yeah, sounds like a laugh.'

'Great,' said Mikey. 'Great.'

It all started out promisingly enough that evening. First Mikey nipped round the community centre and sweet-talked Ernestine into letting him use one of the offices for his audition. Even got Col round to play some piano. Then the girls turned up on time, well, half-nine any-way. That's when things started going to hell.

First problem was finding a song the girls knew and Col could play. Col wanted to do some Motown, 'Heat Wave', 'You Keep Me Hanging On', something like that, but none of the girls seemed to know any of that old-style shit, as they put it. The girls fancied doing 'Survivor' or 'Say My Name', but Col couldn't play either of those. Then the girls had a go a cappella and frankly it sounded hideous. Mikey was no purist, he wasn't expecting the three tenors, but even so, it was horrible. Maybe they just needed the piano. At last he had an idea.

' "*Voulez-vous couchez avec moi?*" '

'You wha?' said three of the girls, before the girl with braids, who was obviously the linguist of the group, weighed in with a hearty 'Fuck off'.

'No,' said Mikey, 'the song, yeah? All Saints, you know?'

The girls nodded. One of them had a go at the opening line.

Mikey looked at Col, raised his eyebrows.

'Yeah, yeah,' said Col, 'Lady Marmalade. I can do that.'

Col basically had one piano part he played on everything – just a question of whether he knew the chords or not. And if he knew the chords well enough, like with this one, well, he could funk it up nicely, and Mikey suddenly had hopes. But then the girls started singing and they immediately dampened down again. There was just no way. None of them could sing a note. Well, the Asian girl wasn't too bad, had a sweet voice, but the rest of them were just bloody painful.

After the second chorus, Col looked at Mikey and Mikey looked back, shaking his head, and Col took the hint and wound the song up.

'Well, what d'you think?' asked Shelley.

Mikey was right on the point of telling them when he caught the Asian-looking girl – Bella, they called her – giving him a bit of a look, bit of an interested look, and he thought, Sod it, bit of sugar-coating never did any harm.

'Nice, girls, nice,' he said, trying not to catch Col's eye. 'Needs a lot of work of course on the harmonies and shit. My man Col here will help you with all that.' He wasn't letting his eyes go anywhere near Col now. 'And you,' he said, looking straight at Bella, 'you've definitely got something. I think we're gonna make you the lead singer, all right, girls?'

The other girls just looked at each other and shrugged.

'So,' Mikey carried on, 'see you here tomorrow night, same time?'

The girls looked at each other some more and giggled. Then the tall girl said, 'Yeah, all right,' and then they were off.

The second they were outside the door Mikey and Col could hear their laughter ringing out down the corridor.

Ten o'clock the next evening and there was no sign of any of the girls. Mikey and Col were just sat in the office, smoking some of Col's finest. Col actually having quite a good time playing the piano, trying to get some jazz–funk thing going, talking to Mikey about buying a sampler – that was one of those things Mikey had heard of, knew they used them on all the records these days, but he didn't have a clue what it was – when Bella popped her head round the door.

'What, they all gone already?' she asked.

'Nah,' said Mikey, 'you're the first one to get here.'

Bella shook her head. 'Fucking typical, all be round Shelley's watching *ER*.'

'So where've you been?' asked Mikey.

'Working, innit,' she said. 'Shop only just closed now.'

And then Mikey had her placed. She worked in the offie over Grangetown. Mum and dad owned it, he supposed. Still, this Bella wasn't one of them good little girls, all training to be chemists or something. She had her hair up in a topknot, Kappa tracksuit and some seriously big trainers. Nice, Mikey liked them sporty.

Bella stood there for a bit, looking unsure what to do next. 'So bit of a waste of time, like, me being here then.'

'Nah,' said Mikey. Then he lowered his voice conspiratorially. 'Fact is, you're the only one can sing anyway.'

'Yeah, you think so?' she said, her face momentarily breaking into a smile. Then she frowned. 'Still, not much point in carrying on now, is there?'

'Course there is,' said Mikey. 'C'mon, sit down. You like a little smoke?'

Bella smiled and nodded, and Col passed her the spliff.

'Look,' said Mikey, 'here's the plan. We do a little work now, figure out what sort of songs really suit your voice, then I'll put some ads around like, audition some more girls, get a little bit of an act going and we'll be ready for the talent night.'

'Talent night?' said Col, as this was the first he'd heard of it.

'Yeah,' said Mikey, who'd half heard something about it on the radio, waiting in the Spar that afternoon, big thing up town, loads of TV people there and stuff. Big chance.

Col shook his head and started playing the piano, unmistakable Stevie Wonder chords this time, and Bella smiled, Col's skunk going straight to the spot. 'Yeah,' she said, 'I knows this one.' And then she started singing, 'You are the sunshine of my life,' sweet as anything, and for the first time Mikey thought he might be on to something.

Next few days Mikey started looking around seriously for some more girls. He asked everyone he knew. He stuck posters up around the place: the community centre, all the shops around Butetown, even went up town and put one in Spillers. Put on the poster for anyone interested to show up the community centre nine o'clock next Tuesday. No phone number 'cause Col wouldn't let Mikey use his mobile number, and there was no way Mikey could risk putting his own phone number on it – Tina would kill him if a whole bunch of girls started phoning up, paranoid as she was. Course paranoid wasn't exactly the word, Mikey had to admit.

Still, by the time Tuesday evening came around, Mikey didn't have a clue what to expect. He made it round the centre about half-eight, had a quick pint of Labatts in the bar talking to a couple of the old boys, when the girls started to show up. By the time Col got there, about ten-past, there were half a dozen of them. There were the Collins twins, dark-skinned girls, bit on the heavy side but Mikey liked the twins angle. There was a white girl called Claire, big girl as well. There was another girl, Maxine, worked as a hairdresser up town, nice girl but never stopped talking. And there were two others.

Frankly Mikey couldn't believe it. He knew he'd done the odd little thing out of line but what the hell had he done to deserve this. First off there was Bobby. Now what he was supposed to do with a gap-toothed lesbian pimp, must be in her thirties but still looked like a teenage boy, he couldn't begin to imagine. And then, for Christ's sake, there was Jan. Yeah, that Jan. His sister.

Now Mikey had nothing against Jan. It was just their worlds didn't collide much these days. He'd see her at work now and again when he had to go down the Health Centre, and they were always friendly like, but her and Tina never hit it off much and, when it came down to it, he knew she disapproved of him, felt he could have done more. He'd got just as many exams as she had; how come she was the one with a job and he was a shoplifter? Still, it was a live-and-let-live kind of thing.

So what the hell was she doing here? She always used to sing around the house and that, but here she was, thirty-two years old and a nurse, bit late for showbiz, he'd have thought. Though, to be fair, stepping back a bit and trying to forget she was his sister like, she looked nice, little bit prim and proper but could be twenty-five easy. And anyway, how old was that fat one who left from the Spice Girls? But hang on, what was he thinking about – the last thing he needed was his bloody family getting stuck into his business.

Now chat was never something Mikey was usually short of, but the next five minutes, waiting for Col and Bella and God knows who else to show up, were bloody

difficult by anybody's standards. Way Mikey played it
was to give Jan a big smile, friendly but professional like,
let her know he was serious, another one for Claire and
Maxine who were busy gabbing together anyway, then
he turned his attention to the twins, gave them a bit of
the old Mikey charm. Twins, he fancied that idea. Bobby
he blanked totally for the while.

Finally, quarter-past nine, Col showed up with Bella,
the pair of them coming through the door together like.

'I was just over Grangetown,' Col said, 'doing a little
bit of business, so I thought I'd stop by the shop, give our
star a lift over like.'

Mikey cut his eyes at Col suspiciously. It wasn't like
Col to offer explanations. Col wasn't paying attention
though. His eyes were busy widening at the sight of the
unlikely gathering he'd walked into.

Mikey decided it was time to take control.

'Right,' he said, 'Col here is going to play and you girls
can take it in turns. We'll hear what you sound like one
at a time and then try you out with Bella here who's
already come through our previous round of auditions.'

Col went over to the piano, started fiddling about and
Mikey went over to the twins. The one on the left,
Danielle if he'd got them right, said they'd like to sing
together, and could they do a gospel tune. So Mikey goes
over to Col and Col starts banging out his usual part, this
time using the chords to the Clark Sisters' 'You Brought
the Sunshine', and the twins smile at each other and
launch into it and they sound terrific, real spine-tingling
stuff.

Mikey found himself breaking out in a big grin, couldn't stop it. After a couple of verses, he waved Bella over and she whispered in his ear she didn't know the song but then she had a go anyway, and they sounded great. Bella had that Diana Ross sexy thing going and the twins had the big harmonies. All it needed, Mikey reckoned, was a soprano, someone with a nice Denise Williams kind of a high voice and they'd be sorted.

Maxine went next. She whispered in Col's ear what she wanted to sing and he shuddered slightly. There was always going to be one wanted to sing 'The Greatest Love of All'. You asked Col there should be a law against it. It was like blokes with guitars in music shops doing 'Smells Like Teen Spirit', shouldn't be allowed. Then Maxine started singing and it was even worse than he expected. She murdered the high notes and hardly even bothered with the low notes. Worst thing was, you could see as she was doing it that, far as she was concerned, Whitney and Mariah could give up now, she, Maxine, was wiping the floor with them.

Bella looked at Mikey, with a pleading expression on her face, as if to say are you going make me try and harmonise with that? Mikey just shook his head. Handled it nicely though, came over to Maxine, put his arm round her, told her she had too much personality to be in a group, she was one of those people born to be a solo act, and he'd certainly be in touch any time that's what he was looking for.

Claire was up next and just asked Col what he fancied playing. Col says how about a little Luther Vandross.

Claire smiles, says yeah, she loves her Luther and Col kicks into 'If Only for One Night', and the second Claire opens her mouth Mikey could tell she was perfect. Lovely high voice and she could really do all that Luther fancy stuff, playing around with the notes and that.

Mikey motioned Bella over and Bella found a part and that was nice and then the twins came in too, but they couldn't find a part so Col stopped the song and started again with 'When Will I See You Again', the old Three Degrees thing.

Bella kicked it off, the twins came in next, then Claire added the high part and it was absolutely blinding. Mikey found himself hopping from leg to leg in excitement. The only cloud on the horizon, far as he could see, was he was going to have to bring in some kind of fitness trainer. One big girl in the group was OK, three was probably pushing it.

Then he was interrupted by his sister tapping him on the shoulder. Bollocks. He'd managed to blot Jan and Bobby out of his mind. Still, what could he do? All they had to do was listen to realise he'd got himself a girl group. He was just about to give her a regretful shrug when the door opened and in walked the twins' grand-mother, Sister Lorraine to her fellow congregationalists, Mrs Collins to Mikey.

Sister Lorraine was fierce. Always had been, and she'd never liked Mikey much. Still blamed him for knocking her favourite niece up, which must have been, Christ, getting on fifteen years ago. Mikey never understood why everyone always seemed to blame him. Fair enough, he knew he strayed around a bit, never knowingly turned down a decent offer and all that, but it takes two to tango and people seemed to forget that.

Anyway, ancient business, water under the bridge and recycled half a dozen times far as he was concerned, but Sister Lorraine took one look at Mikey, took a quick listen to confirm her suspicion that the twins weren't singing no gospel song and then appeared to blow up to twice her normal size, which was formidable enough to start out with. Even before she opened her mouth Col stopped playing and the girls all turned to face her.

'Danielle,' she said, 'Lavine. You call that singing the Lord's praises?'

The twins looked shamefaced at their grandmother and shook their heads.

'No,' said Sister Lorraine. 'Well, let's thank God I got here in time. There is no good at all will come from associating with this man.' She pointed her finger at Mikey. 'Now pick up your coats, children. We going home now.'

And that was that. Half Mikey's group walked straight out the door. Danielle just managed to twist and give Mikey a regretful smile but that was all.

Mikey turned and was just about to tell Bella and Claire not to worry, he would set up some more auditions for next week, replace the twins, no trouble, when he saw Jan walking up with a purposeful look on her face.

'Well,' she said.

Mikey shrugged, smiled weakly and Jan turned to Col. ' "Wishing On a Star," ' she said 'In C.'

Col nodded and started playing. Jan let him get into the swing of it then started singing. And she was OK, not great but perfectly fine. Claire came in after a little while and did the high part beautifully. Then, before Mikey said a word, Bobby started in and after a couple of false starts found a low part. Bella couldn't find much to do, just sang along with Jan really, but once again it was sounding like a group.

Mikey looked across at Col. Col looked back and shrugged his shoulders as if to say it sounded all right with him. They tried out a couple more songs, an old Motown thing, 'Nowhere to Run', that Col suggested and had to teach everybody, then 'Candle in the Bloody Wind' that Bella suggested and Col went along with, which made Mikey even more certain that something was going on.

Still, it sounded nice enough if you forgot what it was and Mikey was just about to call it a day when Jan pulled out a notebook and asked if they'd mind having a go at a song she'd written herself. Mikey nearly had a hernia on the spot but the other girls all went oh great and let's hear it, and so Jan sat down at the piano with Col for a little bit and played him the tune. Five minutes later, Col had managed to adapt his all-purpose piano part and the girls were picking up the harmonies.

Mikey would have put money on it being some piece of save-the-trees nonsense, but instead it was some really sad thing about being dumped, which made Mikey feel a bit guilty he didn't pay more attention to what was going on with her, him being the big brother and everything. And, fair play once again, the song wasn't bad at all.

And after that they did all pack up and Mikey headed round to the Bosun for a quick one, feeling like he'd done a decent night's work after all, and doing his best not to think about the fact that his group now had his sister in it. Not to mention Bobby.

Didn't last long though, the trying not to think thing. He was only halfway through his Labatts when Bobby came in the Bosun and sat down next to him.

'All right, Mikey boy?'

'All right, Bob,' said Mikey reluctantly.

'So how you liking the management game?'

Mikey scanned Bobby's face for signs of sarcasm. She knew as well as he did about his misadventures in the pimping game. Way Mikey saw it the whole thing was screwed up. Girls always got chopsy about handing their money over to some bloke, needed it for his legitimate expenses like, paying the court fines, keeping the coppers sweet, all of that. Hustlers always acted like you were taking their money and sticking it straight up your nose. No sense of the responsibilities at all. But when it came to giving the money over to some other girl, one of the bloody lesbians down there, well, never a dicky bird. And the really ironic thing was, they'd all go on like they were more afraid of some girl like Bobby here, five-foot-three if she was lucky, than they were of the blokes. Screwed up.

'All right,' he said cautiously.

'Safe,' said Bobby, ' 'cause, look, if you needs any help I knows one or two people puts on shows and stuff round the clubs.'

Mikey laughed. 'It's not them kind of shows I'm thinking of. Never seen you as the lap-dancing type anyway, Bob.' Mikey broke off, expecting a laugh from Bobby, but she just frowned instead and Mikey realised she was dead serious about this.

'No,' she said, impatient like, 'it's the same people put on regular shows. Like Bernie Walters – you know him, right?'

Mikey knew of him, as it happened. Bernie Walters had been around the scene since the bloody ark. Used to run the strippers down the Dowlais, but had some places up town and all. So he nodded.

'Yeah, well, Bernie's got this big talent night going. Up the Forum next week.'

Mikey nodded again. 'Yeah,' he said, 'I knows about that. I was thinking of putting the group in for it. If we're ready like.'

'Yeah,' said Bobby, and Mikey couldn't believe it, he could see this dreamy expression taking over Bobby's face. Like she really thought she was going to get up on stage and turn into Mariah Carey. Though, way things were going these days, anything was possible, far as Mikey could see. Look at that Bjork. Fuck was that about, he'd like to know. Still, he was feeling better now he realised Bobby was right into it. Christ, people were easy once you figured out what they wanted.

'Yeah, Bob,' he said, 'that's the plan. Course there's a lot of work to do yet.'

Couple of days later, Mikey's in the Spar, minding his own business. Well, having a little chat with a girl he bumped into there. Just checking out whether she fancied giving the music industry a go, you know, when he gets a firm tap on the shoulder.

Mikey whirls round wondering which fucking copper's going to have a laugh going through the old 'What you got in your pockets' routine. A person got a reputation for something – playing football, say, or shoplifting, come to that – people never let you hear the last of it, even when you were a fully fledged music-biz professional.

So there's Mikey, spinning round ready to go right off on one and then he freezes. Just like that.

'Hiya, Mum,' he says, wondering what the hell's going on. His mum lived over Whitchurch, no need to be in his local Spar. 'So what you doing over here? Come to see Jan?'

Mikey's mum glowered. She wasn't a big woman. You wouldn't have expected her to be, given the sawn-off size of Mikey. But she had presence all right. In her younger days she'd been the spit of Eartha Kitt, same cat's eyes. Still had them, come to that. These days she had the raspy voice too, courtesy of the old Embassy Regals.

'So why didn't you tell me?' she asked, eyes boring straight into Mikey's shiftless soul.

'Say what?'

'About this group of yours, darling?'

Mikey shuddered. She'd started the darling thing sometime in his teens. No one's mother called their kids darling. She must have seen it in one of her films. He braced himself wondering what was coming next.

'Well, Mum,' he said, 'early days, you know what I'm saying.'

'Well,' she said, all smiles now. 'I think it's a fabulous idea. Jan's told me all about it and she agreed you need a little help on the presentation side, you knows.'

'Well, Mum . . .' Mikey attempted to butt in, but to no avail.

'All the dresses and make-up and stuff, styling they calls it. So I says to Jan, don't worry, your mum'll do it for you. So that's settled then?'

'What is?' asked Mikey, his head spinning.

And so it came to pass that on the day of the big talent night at the Forum Mikey was accompanied by his mother, his sister, a lesbian pimp and two teenage shopgirls. If it hadn't been for Col, Mikey would have gone insane days previously.

Still, funny thing was, Mikey was feeling pretty optimistic. The last few days they'd been rehearsing every night and they'd got two songs really well nailed. They were going to do this old Supremes song, 'Up the Ladder to the Roof', and then they were going to do Jan's song and, to be honest, Mikey thought they had to be in with a chance. Didn't sound bad at all.

Even his mum had turned out OK, done a lovely job

on the make-up. Sorted out the outfits too, which had looked like being a problem. Mikey had reckoned they should all dress the same, like those old-time groups, but that had never looked like working, you'd have had to shoot Bobby to get her in a dress. So Lena, Mikey's mum, had come through, said they should go with a Spice Girls kind of thing, give them all different images like.

So Bella went street, in her tracksuit and big trainers. Jan went roots in some kind of African print thing and her hair in a turban. Claire was the tarty one. Nice big girl like you, Lena said, got to be proud of yourself, let them see what you got, and stuck her in a bra top she was practically exploding out of. Worked for Mikey anyway, he could hardly take his eyes off her. And then there was Bobby who was wearing some kind of karate outfit, looking mad as fuck, but what the hell.

Still, Mikey was feeling pretty hopeful on the way over to the Forum: him, Col, the four girls and Mikey's mum, who, not to be outdone, was wearing an outrageous leopard-look two-piece, all squeezed into Col's clapped out Audi. They parked in some little staff car park, then trooped round the front attracting some pretty lively looks from the kids standing around outside the Odeon.

It was only when they were actually inside the club talking to the TV people organising the show that Mikey discovered the big screw-up.

'Hello,' says the woman, some kind of Nazi blonde in heels.

'Hiya,' says Mikey.

'Oh right, hi,' says the woman like she could give a shit. 'So who are you lot being?'

'What?' says Mikey.

'Mis-Teeq? Destiny's Child? Please don't say Spice Girls.'

'No,' says Mikey, 'these here are called Tiger Princess.'

'Yes, I'm sure,' says the Nazi, 'but who are they being?'

Mikey looks baffled once more and the woman shakes her head and says, 'You do realise this is a *Stars in their Eyes* audition, don't you? You know the idea is you impersonate a pop star? Yes?'

Mikey just stood there for a moment. 'Oh yeah, right.'

The woman sighed theatrically. 'Look,' she said, 'I've got other people to check in – why don't you sit over there and work out what you're doing.'

And with that she swivelled round, banishing Mikey utterly from her presence. Her gaze immediately fell on Mikey's mum. She beamed.

'Oh wonderful,' she said. 'Eartha Kitt.'

Ten minutes later Mikey accepted they were screwed. There never had been a girl group with two black girls, one Asian girl and a white girl, far as he knew. Funny thing was the girls themselves didn't seem too bothered.

'Look,' said Mikey, 'I'll go over, have a word, see if they'll let you have a shot at being the Spice Girls.' Desperate idea but there it was.

So Mikey went over, had a word with the Nazi who practically laughed in his face, just pointed around the room where there were at least four sets of Spice Girls who actually looked the part.

Crestfallen, Mikey headed back towards the bar, looking for his crew, who seemed to have disappeared. Eventually he found them out by the cloakroom, and immediately he smelled a rat.

Col was sat on the floor, his keyboard balanced on his lap, banging out the backing to Eartha Kitt's 'Just an Old-fashioned Girl' while Lena practised her purr and the girls did some oohs and aahs in the background.

Mikey looked at Jan and she looked back at him.

'It's a fucking set-up, innit?'

Jan did her best to look innocent but after a couple of seconds she just burst out laughing.

'Well,' said Jan eventually, 'Mum always was a bit of a star. Best thing we give her a hand.'

And so, half an hour later, Mrs Lena Thompson, fifty-eight, of Whitchurch, was waiting next in line for her audition, flanked by hell's own girl group and her devoted son, and accompanied by Col. She was wearing the same leopard-look two-piece she'd turned up to the show in. Coincidence? Mikey was definitely starting to wonder, but what the hell.

The bloke in front was wearing a black suit and heavy black shades. Had to be Roy Orbison and so he was, bloke had the voice down perfect and everything. Only weird thing was after a couple of verses Mikey realised he was singing in Welsh. About the same time the TV people seemed to clock it too and the music stopped and the clipboard Nazi came over.

'Lovely,' she said, 'perfect. Only thing is what language was that you were singing in?'

'Cymraeg,' said the bloke and the TV woman went back and talked to her boss, came back a minute later and said I'm sorry but you have to sing in English on this show. Bloke just looked her up and down, started cussing her out in Welsh and walked straight out the club. Respect, thought Mikey.

And then it was Lena's turn.

'Got your tape, dear?' asked the director.

'Tape?' said Lena. 'Eartha Kitt does not use backing tapes, Eartha Kitt has an accompanist!' and she waved at Col.

Col smiled and bowed.

Lena carried on. 'Meet my musical director, a gentleman of many talents.' She'd got the purr down to a T now. 'Mr Colin . . . Colin –' Lena looked at Col, having forgotten what his surname was. Col leaned over and whispered in her ear.

'Yes, my verry, verry good friend and accompanist, Mr Colin X. Now' – she held her hand out to the assistant director – 'lead me to the stage.'

It hardly needs saying what happened next. Lena was a knockout, of course. She got the best applause of the night, along with one of the sets of Spice Girls, but then the producer went into a huddle with the director, talking about the show's demographics and Saturday-night wrinklies, and Lena was pronounced the winner.

She'd made it through to the first of the TV rounds, shooting up in London in a couple of months.

Afterwards, Mikey went backstage to give the old girl his best.

'You'll be needing a manager then, Mum,' he said.

'Yes, Mikey,' she said. And then she turned round and waved to a heavily sun-tanned feller, about her own age. 'And here he is, Mr Bernie Walters.'

Still, it wasn't all bad. The Bernie feller turned out OK, said he'd seen Mikey's girls and he didn't know if he had any work for singers but any of them fancied doing a bit of dancing down the Dowlais on a Wednesday night, specially the big girl, he'd see Mikey right for a cut.

Mikey said he'd see what he could do. Got to start at the bottom after all.

MIKEY'S LAST TANGO

Mikey was sitting in his brief's waiting room – little matter of a couple of non-payments, nothing heavy – trying to focus his attention on a copy of *FHM*, when he realised he was starting to get a little tired of life. There were a few reasons why that he could point to. He'd turned forty a few months back, not a birthday he'd drawn anyone's attention to. Specially seeing Tina had got it into her head that he was only thirty-nine, which he hadn't corrected her about but made him feel a bit odd.

So there was that, just simply getting older was enough to bring anyone down a bit. Then there was Mikey Junior who was growing up fast. You wouldn't think you'd miss something boring like walking your kid to school every morning but, now little Mikey was going off by himself, Mikey couldn't help feeling he was getting a bit unnecessary.

And then there was his eyesight. Mikey was starting to have to face it: he needed glasses. Other week he'd been doing his patented five-bottle shuffle at the perfume counter in Howell's. A little routine he has where the girl on the counter's got half the perfumes in the store out for Mikey to sniff and he generates such confusion that in the end they never notice when one slips into his pocket. Well, the old manual dexterity had been there last time he tried it but this time he'd got the wrong bottle – the eau de toilette and not the parfum he'd got the order for.

And why was that? Because the writing was too small for him to read these days without holding it up about an inch from his face, which might look just a little bit suspicious. No, there was nothing for it, he was going to have go down the optician's, get himself sorted out. And of course it wasn't a big deal and it wasn't that Mikey was vain exactly. It was just pure unavoidable proof the he wasn't what anyone would call young any more.

He was getting older all right and the world was changing. Still, there was one thing Mikey knew could reliably take your mind off these kind of feelings. He put the copy of *FHM* down, waited till a couple of Somali boys had sat themselves down, then turned his attention to the receptionist, nice little red-haired piece, ran a few lines past her, then cut to the chase.

'So how's about we have a drink then, you and me?'

'Yeah,' she said, just like that. 'Sure, tell you what, I'm going down Amigos tomorrow lunchtime. Why don't you come down, 'bout half-twelve.'

'Sweet,' said Mikey, and headed in to see Stuart the brief, feeling like he had a renewed appetite for life.

★　　★　　★

So next day, half-twelve, Mikey's still feeling pleased with himself. He'd persuaded Tina that Stuart had told him he needed to come back again and she'd bought it for once. Actually that was another thing that was bringing him down – didn't seem like Tina was as jealous as she used to be. Anyway, there he is walking into Amigos, already visualising the way things are going to go – couple of drinks and back round to Katy's for a little afternoon business. And then he opens the door and right away he can see he's got it all wrong.

He told Col about it later on, standing in the bookie's watching the four-thirty from Doncaster.

'So I walks in there,' he said, 'and she's only sat round with half a dozen of her mates all watching the bastard football, wearing the shirts and all. And that's just the girls, Col. Girls! What's up with that?'

Col shook his head, smiling, keeping his eyes on the racing.

Mikey carried on, waxing indignant. 'Old days, Col, I used to love a good match: rugby international, FA Cup Final, whatever. Kick-off three o'clock you know all the fellers will be down the pub watching it. So five-past three you knocks on the back door, goes oh hiya, love, Barry in, or whatever – that's just an example, I don't mean any particular Barry – and the girl goes oh no the boring bastard's off watching the football, and you goes oh I hates football, don't know what they sees in it, and then she's making you a cup of tea and you've got ninety minutes to work the Mikey magic.'

'Plus extra time if you're lucky,' says Col.

'Yeah,' says Mikey, 'not to mention the penalty shoot-out.' And he laughed again before a cloud passed over his face. 'But now, Col, all the bloody women, well, the young ones anyway, they're all in the pub watching it too – not bloody natural.'

'Well,' says Col, 'you'll just have to pretend to take an interest and all.'

'Yeah,' says Mikey, 'well, that's what I figured the other day. You know, you can't beat 'em join 'em kind of thing. So we're all sat in there, me and this girl, Katy, and all these other mates of hers, and they're all going like, "Who d'you fancy, Mikey?" and I'm like just about to say, "You, darling," when I can see that'll go down like a lead balloon and so I'm looking at the big screen and there a bunch of blond geezers lined up and a bunch of African geezers so I says the African fellers.'

'Senegal,' chips in Col. 'Sweden Senegal.'

'Yeah,' says Mikey, 'whatever. Anyway seemed like that was the right answer 'cause all the girls are going yeah go Senegal so I'm like yeah and then we're all sat down for bloody hours watching this shit.'

'Good game it was.'

'Take your word for it, seemed to go on for bastard ever, and that was just the first half. Then they cut to the commentators and that chopsing on about what's going to happen next and I think, Well, now's my chance. So I start running a few lines past this Katy and she's like, "You mind saving it for later, I'm trying to listen to the analysis." Analysis, Col! It's a joke, I'm telling you. So anyway I've had enough of this, say I'll catch her later and she just goes, "Yeah, bye." Doesn't even take her eyes off the screen.'

'Yeah?' says Col, shaking his head slightly in practised sorrow as his six to one prospect faded in the final furlong and trailed in fifth. 'So what did you do after, then?'

'Oh,' said Mikey, 'little bit of business, nothing much.'

Which wasn't strictly true. After the Katy debacle, Mikey had been walking back through town, feeling unaccountably pissed off. It wasn't just that Katy hadn't rolled over right away. Mikey was a patient man, and he knew the value of persistence in romantic matters. It was just the getting-old thing again, he supposed, feeling like it wasn't his world any more, he didn't know the runnings. Whatever.

To snap himself out of it, and make sure the visit to town wasn't a complete waste of time, he decided to fill a couple of orders. First one went fine, couple of sweatshirts from Gap. He even stopped to sign the petition a bunch of students had going outside asking people not to shop there 'cause they exploited their workforce or whatever. Made Mikey feel like he was doing a public service, really.

Next stop was the department store. Mikey liked department stores, so much space to create a little confusion. He hit the menswear first then the women's and it all seemed to be going so easy he got a little bit cocky. Went over to the shoe department, tried on a pair of top-of-the-range Timberlands, fitted him nicely. Wasn't an order, he just fancied a pair for himself. So then he asked for three or four more pairs to try in different styles. Ended up with shoes everywhere and Mikey casually putting on the first pair he'd tried like they were his own shoes, and then walking away.

He'd left it at that he'd probably have been OK, but instead he remembered one more thing he'd been asked for, couple of Diesel shirts in kids' sizes. And it was just as he was about to slip them in his bag that he notices the fit young feller casually standing behind him. Store detective to the life. Mikey has learnt over the years that discretion is the better part of valour so he put the kids' shirts down, picks up the first shirt he sees in an adult size and heads over to the changing room where he unloads all the stuff he's got so far, cursing as he does so. Hundred and fifty quid he'd have got for it easy, but there you go. He walks out of the changing room, hands the shirt back to the assistant, and saunters out of the main doors.

Two seconds later the casual young feller has got Mikey by the collar. Mikey turns round looking outraged. Hell do you want? Store detective says I believe you have stolen blah blah. Mikey laughs in his face, opens his shopping bag, look, mate, I've got nothing. Store detective smiles and looks down at Mikey's feet. Mikey looks down too. Oh Jesus Christ, he's still got the Timberlands on.

'Fuck you looking at my feet for?' he says.

'I've reason to believe you haven't paid for those shoes, sir.'

'They're my bastard shoes,' says Mikey loudly, hoping to draw some passers-by into matters, cause a little distraction.

'Sir, let's go inside and sort this out, shall we?'

Mikey casts his eyes around looking for an ally on the street. Nobody there, in fact the streets seem a lot quieter than normal. And just as he's thinking that he hears a big roar from the sports bar across the street – bloody football must still be going on. The store detective's grip suddenly loosens. Must be a football fan wondering what's going on, thinks Mikey in the split second it takes him to duck down and thrust his whole bodyweight backwards into the store detective, causing him to topple over and giving Mikey the two seconds he needs to make a break for it.

Mikey headed straight round the corner and into the arcades. He loved the arcades. In no time he was in the Morgan Arcade just where it splits into two by the café. He could hear the store detective charging along behind him but he didn't look back, he faked to go left, started to go right, and then darted into the alley led through to the Royal Arcade, then, just at the end of the alley, instead of making the obvious move and carrying on into the Royal, he nipped into David Morgan's, walked very fast over to the stairs then kept on going up till he got to the rooftop café. Got himself a can of Sprite and sat down outside on the terrace, feeling about as cool as. Mikey pulls it off again.

He stayed up in the café for twenty minutes, long enough for the store detective to get fed up with looking around for him, then headed back downstairs, after lifting a little present for that Katy just to show he wasn't rattled or anything.

Except that, he realised now, talking to Col, he was

rattled. He was feeling old and he was feeling like he couldn't hack it any more. Those few seconds when the store detective had had him by the collar, he'd just thought, Prison, I can't face that again. He'd done it once, when he was younger. Three months. Hadn't been too bad – he'd been young and he'd had some mates in with him. Coped all right. Now though he just felt like he wasn't coping at all any more.

'Look, Col,' he said, 'got to go,' and Col said, 'Yeah, later,' not paying attention, watching the horses line up for the five o'clock, last race of the day, hoping for a last-minute reprieve, not expecting one.

Back outside Mikey found himself just wandering around for a bit, before his feet, by force of habit, led him home.

Inside the flat in the seconds between opening the door and Tina and little Mikey registering his presence, he had time to imagine how nice it might be if he was just a regular geezer coming home from his proper job and Tina was just a nice housewife getting his tea ready for when he walked in.

Took about five more seconds for it to be royally confirmed that this wasn't the way things were. Little Mikey was in the living room with a bunch of his mates, all of them yelling their heads off, arguing about whose mobile ringtones were the coolest. Tina was on the regular phone chopsing on to her mum, and Mikey could smell the oven chips burning from out in the hall.

He chucked the chips in the bin, gave little Mikey two

quid to go down the chip shop and take his mates with him, then he was just about to start yelling at Tina when she finally got off the phone except she got hers in first.

Where'd he been? Didn't he know she was meant to take her mum down the health centre while he looked after little Mikey? Thoughtless bloody bastard, blah, blah. And where had he been, she'd like to know. No, don't tell her, she knew all right – with some thick bloody slag didn't know a loser when she saw one.

Well, it wasn't like Mikey hadn't heard all this and worse a hundred, no a bloody thousand, times before. Except mostly he'd at least done something to be guilty about and normally he wasn't so tired and maybe it was just hot in the flat or something but, be honest, it was all he could do not to burst into tears, just felt like a little kid getting told off by his mum.

'Look,' he said weakly, 'I was just working in town like.'

'Oh yeah?' she said. 'Well, what have you got then?'

'Nothing,' he said. 'I almost got bloody nicked, didn't I?'

'Bollocks,' she said, 'you were never anywhere near fucking town, you been round some tart's house, I fuckin' knows it.'

'No,' he said weakly, unable to defend himself, just repeated it again, 'no,' and Tina looked at him and he could see she didn't know whether to be worried about him or go in for the kill.

'Look,' he said, 'look, I've got the bag here,' and he pulled a shopping bag out of his inside jacket pocket, ready to show it to her empty, and as he did so he felt something like salvation inside it.

'Look,' he said, 'calm down, Teen. I bought you a present.'

'You what?' she said, now looking as if she couldn't decide whether to hit him or have him committed.

'Yeah,' he said and he pulled out the eau de toilette he'd lifted by mistake the other day and handed it to Tina.

She took it from him like he was handing her a live grenade, made as if to put it down without smelling it but at the last moment she changed her mind, sprayed a little bit on her wrist and sniffed it, and as she did so her face changed, softened.

'Christ,' she said, 'I'd never have thought you remembered.'

'What's that?'

'Don't what's that me, this is the perfume I always used to wear back when we were first going out. You remember it?'

And with that she raised her wrist to Mikey's nose and he smelt it and he did remember and at the exact same time some other part of his brain was hearing Sugar Minott singing 'Good Thing Going' and he was twenty-two years old in the Casablanca Club and Tina was a fit eighteen-year-old he'd had his eye on for a couple of weeks and the world was not exactly at his feet but it was all ahead of him.

And now, holding Tina's hand, smelling teenage Tina and pissed-off thirty-five-year-old Tina at the same time, he knew that life was behind him as much as in front of him – the Casablanca Club was long gone, he hadn't heard the sweet sound of Sugar Minott in years – but he was still here and Tina was still with him. And he was the same person who'd seen her at the Casa B, had walked over and said, 'Darlin', you fancy a little dance?' And now he found himself absent-mindedly saying those very words to her.

'Yeah,' said Tina, lit up and laughing, now just as then. 'I do.'

And in the absence of a dance floor they held each other close and danced around the kitchen.

A CHILD'S CHRISTMAS IN SPLOTT PART 2

Little Mikey was wandering around Splott Market, waiting for his dad to get finished with talking to the lady ran a stall sold these little bottles of aroma stuff, meant to make you feel good. Most pointless stall in the whole place far as Little Mikey could see.

Little Mikey was meant to be looking for Christmas presents. Well, actually they both were, him and his dad who was called Mikey as well, that's why everyone called Little Mikey Little Mikey, which was getting on his nerves a bit now he was nine and he was thinking of telling everyone to call him Michael, but anyway that wasn't the point right now. The point was that they were meant to be there buying something for his mum, Tina, that's her name, but all they've done so far is have bacon rolls and then his dad met this aroma woman and right away he can see what's going to happen, she comes up and gives dad a big kiss and then whispers something in his ear. Probably, Little Mikey reckons, she's one of his dad's old girlfriends from before he met mum, 'cause he used to have a lot of girlfriends then.

So anyway, next thing that happens is dad says just give us five minutes, you have a look round see if there's anything you want. So that's what he's doing. Mostly there's just loads of clothes stalls full of brands you never heard of or things that even look fake to Little Mikey and he figures something that looks fake to a nine-year-old definitely can't be good news. There's a couple of stalls selling mobile-phone covers and he has a bit of a look at them, but his phone's his dad's old one so it's really big and there's no covers there that fit it, they're all for the 3210 and 3310. Funny thing is though, he's just looking at the phone covers and his phone rings. He picks it up and it's his mum.

'Hiya, love,' she says.

He says, 'Hiya,' back and wonders why she always rings him when he's out with his dad. Why doesn't she ring his dad's phone? Maybe it's not working properly or something.

'You got anything yet, love?' she says. 'Oh no, don't tell me. Listen, is dad there? I needs a word with him.'

'Oh,' says little Mikey, 'he's just over at another stall talking to his friend.'

'Oh yeah,' says his mum, sounding all interested, 'which friend is it? Do I know him?'

'No,' says little Mikey, 'it's not a him, it's a her. She's got her own stall.'

'Oh,' says his mum, 'that's nice, love. Anyway how about you tells him to give me a ring soon as he's finished talking, all right?' Then his mum clicks her phone off, not even waiting for him to say goodbye.

So Little Mikey walks back to where his dad is but he's still busy talking so he wanders off in the other direction where some auctioneer guy is standing up on the side of a lorry with a load of boxes showing everyone all these toys like you get in Hypervalue, big robots and stuff that you just know will turn to crap as soon as you get them out the box, but the feller's talking about how you got all these toys together they'd cost you £130, which Little Mikey frankly doubts, but he's selling them for £20 the lot which does sound like quite a good deal, and all these people are putting their hands up and so he runs off to get his dad 'cause it seems like he at least ought to see what's going on and maybe they'd have some ladies' stuff in a bit so they could get something nice for mum, 'cause by the sound of it she could do with a bit of cheering up.

So he's back again and he can't believe it but his dad's still talking to this aroma woman – maybe he's signing up to buy some stuff for mum or something – and Little Mikey's pretty sure the lady must have been an old girlfriend or something of Dad's 'cause he's standing right up close to her and he's got his hand on her back, stroking up and down like.

Anyway, Little Mikey reckons this is hot news he's bringing, so he calls out, 'Dad, you got to see these toys they got over the auction.'

And his dad turns round and he's smiling but Little Mikey can tell he's not too keen to come look. 'Yeah?' he says. 'Anything good?'

'No,' says Little Mikey truthfully, 'but I was thinking for mum . . .'

'Yeah, go on,' says the aroma lady to his dad, 'you should have a look.'

His dad gets out of it, though, by saying, 'Tell you what, son, you go and have a look and as soon as they got some ladies' stuff you think your mum'd like, you come and get me, yeah?'

'All right,' says Little Mikey, but he's getting a bit bored now and when he gets over by the auction it's getting really crowded and uncomfortable so instead he walks around some more till he ends up in the outside part of the market and there's a stall selling computer games and stuff so Little Mikey has a good look at that.

There's nothing good for the Playstation there but to be honest Little Mikey's getting a bit bored with his Playstation. All the best games are for Playstation 2 now and he doesn't have one of them, but what they do have is a bunch of PC games and programs and he's been getting well into his PC lately.

'Have you got Dreamweaver?' he asks the bloke, cause all of a sudden he's decided what he really wants for Christmas is a really good graphics program to do a website with.

But the bloke just looks at him and says, 'What's that, son, Dreamweaver? I dunno, I might have it back at my shop,' and Little Mikey can tell he's never heard of Dreamweaver, just sells these crappy old Windows 95 games all cost about £5 and Dreamweaver costs loads and they'd never have it on a stall like this and his dad probably couldn't afford to buy it him for Christmas, and anyway he could probably just get the demo off a magazine, and then he'd heard you could get like a code breaker or something would let you convert the demo into the real thing and it wouldn't cost nothing, but just once, Little Mikey thought, he would like to have the whole package in the right big box with the manual and everything.

Nothing in Little Mikey's house ever seemed to come in the right box. His dad was always getting stuff from his mates or someone in a pub. And there always seemed to be bits missing and stuff, like when they got the PC it didn't come with any leads or a keyboard or anything, which seemed a bit funny.

Thinking about this is making Little Mikey feel fed up so this time he heads back to find his dad and he's not going to be fobbed off again. But when he gets there he can't believe his dad is still chatting to this woman and now if he didn't know better he'd think they'd just been kissing 'cause when he comes up and says, 'Hi, Dad,' they both like jump apart a bit and his dad digs in his pocket like he's going to give him some money to go and get a drink or something and Little Mikey's just about to say I don't want a drink I want to go, when this other lady comes up and she's obviously a friend of the aroma lady and she's got big hair extensions which Little Mikey thinks look quite cool and she and the aroma lady do all this kiss kiss, how you doing, darling, stuff then the extensions lady looks at Mikey Senior and you can tell she's not one of dad's old girlfriends 'cause she gives him a bit of a look, and dad gives her a bit of a look back and the extensions lady says, 'What's he doing here?' which Little Mikey thinks sounds a bit rude, and then his dad says, 'C'mon, son, let's go,' and Little Mikey forgets about it 'cause now he's got his dad back to himself.

And so they're walking round the market together, laughing and joking a bit like they normally do when they're together, and Little Mikey shows his dad this ice-hockey shirt that he likes and his dad has a look at it and has a word with the man runs the stall and then comes back and says well, make sure you tell Santa about that, and Little Mikey laughs to show he's known for years there's no such thing as Santa but he's also big enough to see how it's nice to pretend there is.

And then they find this stall which has got all these kind of Egyptian carvings like Tutankhamen's head and stuff and his dad says, 'You think mum would like one of these?' and Little Mikey remembers something.

'Oh,' he said, 'Mum rang up when you were talking to that lady.'

'Oh yeah,' said his dad. 'What did she want?'

'Talk to you, Dad, but I said you were busy.'

Mikey Senior smiled but you could see he didn't think anything was funny. 'OK,' he said, 'I'll bell her in a minute,' and then he asks the lady on the stall how much the Tutankhamen thing is and just then Little Mikey's phone rings again.

'Oh hi,' he says. It's his mum again. 'Dad's here now. He was just going to ring you.'

'Oh yeah,' says his mum, like she doesn't believe him.

'Yeah, he was,' says Little Mikey, 'it's just he's trying to get your present,' thinking that should make her happy, but she just says, 'Well, is he there then?' and Little Mikey gives the phone to his dad and he starts talking on the phone and straight away Little Mikey can tell they're having a row, and somehow he can't help feeling like it's his fault.

When his dad comes off the phone, Little Mikey can tell right away he's gone into a bad mood. 'All right,' he says, 'let's go up town – I've had enough of this place,' and he just leads the way off and little Mikey looks back and sees the Tutankhamen woman looking at them, like what did I do wrong, and something about that makes Little Mikey feel a bit sad so he just turns round and follows after his dad into the car park and his uncle Del's car, a beat-up old Datsun.

His dad was always saying he was going to get a car, be pointing at his mate Kenny's new Audi saying, 'What d'you think about getting one of those, Junior,' and Little Mikey would laugh and say, 'Yeah, wicked,' and one time back when he was in Year Four he'd actually told his mates in school that his dad was going to buy one – it wasn't an Audi that time it was a Mercedes 7 series.

And this other kid, Jermaine, had laughed at him and said, 'How's that, my mum says your dad's just a shoplifter,' and Little Mikey had had to fight him at playtime, and afterwards he'd had to see the head and then she called his mum in and she'd given him a row till he told her what the kid had said to him and then she said

Jermaine was just saying it 'cause he was jealous 'cause he'd never even seen his dad.

And that made little Mikey feel a bit better but still now he hated it whenever his dad said that thing about cars 'cause he knew it wasn't going to come true. It was like Santa, it was one of those stories grown-ups told you.

He cheered up a bit once they got into town though. Dad parked round the back of the shops somewhere where there were loads of vans and it was all double yellow lines, but dad said that didn't matter on a Sunday, so they went and had a look round the shops.

Little Mikey was keeping an eye out for Dreamweaver but he didn't see it anywhere though he did see The Sims which his friend Lee had got and he told his dad he'd like that and his dad made a little note of it in his book. And then they looked in JJB Sports and Little Mikey saw a Cardiff City shirt which he said would be OK when his dad asked him, though he wasn't that bothered really and he hoped he didn't get it, at least not for Christmas.

And then they saw a Nike jacket that Little Mikey said Mum might like and his dad said yeah and ruffled his hair and Little Mikey felt good about that but his dad didn't buy it right off, just wrote it down in his book, said there was too much of a queue at the moment, he'd come back in the week.

Then they went past this shop called Lush and Little Mikey said, 'Let's have a look in here for Mum.' He thought of that 'cause lush was his mum's favourite word at the moment which was a bit embarrassing really 'cause it was what all the girls in school said, but anyway. So they went in there and it was all make-up and stuff and they had a Christmas gift set of stuff all wrapped up which looked nice and his dad wrote that down in his book too, even though there wasn't much of a queue this time.

And then they were walking through this arcade Little Mikey couldn't remember going down before and there was a computer shop, more of a professional one not just a games place, and they went in there and his dad asked the man if they had Dreamweaver and he said he did and it was two hundred and something pounds and his dad whistled but he wrote it down in his book anyway.

But then, when they were out of the shop, Little Mikey had a terrible thought. He thought, What if Jermaine was telling the truth, what if dad is a shoplifter and he goes back there and he tries to shoplift Dream-weaver and he gets caught and 'cause it's really expensive they'll probably send him to prison. And he says, 'Oh, Dad, I don't want that Dreamweaver, you won't get it for me, will you, Dad?' and he couldn't stop his voice from almost breaking like he's going to start crying but his dad doesn't notice, just says, 'No worries, junior,' and then a phone rings.

Dad's this time, and straight away Little Mikey can hear it's Mum again and they have another row and it ends up with Dad saying, 'Shut the fuck up, woman, I'll be back in ten minutes, and you can have a go at me then,' and then he drives back really fast and not saying anything and when they get there Mum looks at them and says, 'So where's the shopping then?'

And before he can hear what Dad tells her, Little Mikey runs into his room and shuts the door and he turns the computer on with the sound up loud but he can still hear them shouting, and then they go in the bedroom, probably so he can't hear them, but they're still making noises, only when he comes out later on for his tea they're looking all happy together again, which is weird.

The whole of the week before Christmas he tried to think what was safe to ask for, something he was sure his dad wouldn't steal and get into trouble for. He couldn't think of anything apart from asking for something really big like an elephant but what on earth would he want an elephant for? All the things he did want were pretty small really.

Finally on the Saturday before Christmas he goes into town again with his dad, his mum going, 'C'mon, Mikey, you sort the boy out with something nice,' but he still can't think what to get. So he ends up just pointing at all these stupid things like a silver football he sees outside a sports shop only costs three quid and a special-offer *Simpsons* video in HMV and a couple of other things he doesn't really want at all and even a stupid *Harry Potter* pencil case which he hates, but when his dad pointed at it he was just starting to feel so miserable about the whole business, so desperate to get it over with, that he just says yeah that's nice.

After that though he can't take any more so he says, 'How about Mum's present, I've got an idea what she might like,' so they go off and do that and that made

Little Mikey feel a bit better but he supposed his dad has noticed something's up with him 'cause they're walking back home towards Butetown, past the new Cinema the UGC, and Little Mikey's dad says, 'You want to go see the film then, now you're getting the pencil case,' and Little Mikey says, 'Yeah, OK,' so they end up watching *Harry Potter* which is about this kid whose parents are dead and afterwards he holds on to his dad's hand as they walk back home where his mum's like where the hell have you been and she's in a bad mood with dad again . . .

So then it's Christmas Day and for the first time Little Mikey doesn't wake up early, he just wakes up his usual time like it was a school day or something, except there's the pillowcase at the end of the bed. He'd kind of wanted to stay awake to catch his mum or dad bring it in because even though you knew Santa didn't exist it would still be funny to catch your dad carrying the presents in, but he must have fallen asleep first 'cause there was the pillow-case and he starts opening the presents 'cause it's always fun to open stuff, even if you know all it's going to be is like a pencil case and stuff, and then he goes in to see his mum and dad and it's obvious that they've just been kissing, and his mum's looking really happy and she's wearing the chain that Little Mikey told his dad she'd like 'cause he'd seen her looking at it one time in town.

And he says, 'Oh that looks nice, Mum,' and she smiles and his dad says, 'Yeah, love, it was Little Mikey's idea,' and she laughs and hugs him and then she opens the other presents his dad has got her, and he's got the

Nike jacket and the basket of stuff from Lush and the Shaggy CD and everything and Little Mikey feels it's going to be a really nice Christmas after all, even if all he's getting is a silver football.

But then when his dad says, 'Go and have a look under the tree, junior, get your present,' he sees there's two presents there. There's one that's obviously the football but there's also another one that looks like a box, so Little Mikey takes them both into the bedroom and first he opens the football and goes yeah, great, thanks, and then he opens the other package and it's Dreamweaver. In the proper box and everything, so his dad must have gone out and bought it, mustn't he?

But he still can't stop himself from saying, 'Dad, how did you get that? It costs a fortune.'

And his dad smiles and pretends to wave a wand like someone out of *Harry Potter* and says, 'I'm a wizard, aren't I?' and Little Mikey thinks about it and decides that'll do for him. One thing he's starting to notice in life, there's some mysteries you don't want to know the answer to.

THE COLONEL

THE TRANSPORTER BRIDGE

The Colonel had got to know Newport quite well over the years. Used to come over regular to use the bookies back when he still had the forecasting gift and the Cardiff bookies were banning him. And he'd come over now and again, in time of famine, to pick up some draw from a feller he knew, lived round by TJ's.

Spent a whole day there a year or two back, when they had the trouble with the passports, just hanging around waiting to get his renewed. Wasn't too much of a hardship though. He liked the town centre. Liked it better than Cardiff these days, to be honest. Thing was, it reminded him of the way Cardiff used to be – quieter, not so much money being chucked around. Cheaper too. There was this bookshop where everything cost a quid, new books and all. He'd stocked up on film books in there. He liked film books, came in dead handy for the quiz nights.

He was partial to a quiz was the Colonel, another thing that brought him over to Newport now and again.

Quizzes weren't as popular as they used to be. He blamed *Millionaire* for that. Overkill and it made people greedy. Long as it was just a bit of a laugh, put one over on your mates, win enough money to pay for your beer, it was fine. Once you got people spending a grand on phone calls just trying to get on the show – which seemed to be on every time you turned on the bastard telly – well, you could tell it was going to end in tears, couldn't you?

Anyway, Newport, that's where he was heading, sitting on the train, coming up to the Brynglas Tunnel. Reminded him of years back coming over with the lads when he was still playing for the City, over to Scamps on Stow Hill for a lunchtime session with half a dozen strippers thrown in. Jesus, was it really thirty years ago?

Getting off the train, he tried to focus on the job in hand. What he had to do was go see his niece, Jade. Find out what on earth was going on. Liz – his sister, Jade's mum – was going nuts. Jade had phoned up the week before, told Liz she was pregnant. Liz had gone ballistic, said she wasn't having her daughter screw up her life the way she had, practically ordered her to have an abortion on the spot – which even the Colonel could see wasn't the most tactful way of carrying on – and Jade had hung up on her, left her mobile on voicemail any time Liz called back.

So Liz had spent the last few days applying the old moral blackmail to her brother, which she'd been a dab hand at ever since they were kids. 'She'll listen to you,' 'She really looks up to you, you know' – all of that stuff, and finally the Colonel had given in, said he'd go over and see her.

Which was what he was doing now, crossing over the road, past the multi-storey, and heading past the Passport Office to John Frost Square. And he was dreading it. It was one thing being the lovable old rascal of an uncle, he could manage that all right. Lovable rascal of a dad too, he'd managed that and all. Well, Helen, his ex, probably wouldn't agree about that, specially the lovable part, but the kids were doing fine, both grown now.

He was on John Frost Square now, depressing windy bloody bit of municipal design, full of scallies in trackies and Burberry caps. He hurried on towards Pill, just wanting to get this thing over with.

Jade's address turned out to be just off Commercial Street in Pill. The Colonel liked Pill. Same way Newport town centre was like Cardiff used to be, Pill was a bit like Butetown used to be – proper old-fashioned docks community full of all sorts. The house itself was in a side street, next door to a closed-down tattoo parlour. The Colonel paused outside for a moment, wondering how anyone could fail to make a go of a tattoo parlour these days, when everyone and her nan had a tat. Maybe they'd moved to larger premises.

He shook his head, time to get on with his mission. He knocked on Jade's door. Waited, knocked on the door again. Finally the curtain twitched and a few seconds later the door was flung open and there was Jade smiling and hugging him.

'Uncle Ronnie, what are you doing here?' Then

suddenly she stepped back, a cloud over her face. 'Oh, she sent you, didn't she?'

The Colonel – he'd thank you not to call him Ronnie unless you're family – felt awful. He stood there trying to think of something reasonable to say, looking at his nineteen-year-old niece, dark and pretty in a sulky sort of way, dressed in a grey Adidas tracksuit, no visible sign of any pregnancy.

'She's worried about you,' he said finally, like that might be news.

'She don't have to be,' said Jade, 'just needs to leave me alone.'

They stood there on the doorstep for a bit. Jade chewing her bottom lip and looking sulkier by the second, the Colonel feeling more useless by the second.

'Any chance of a cup of tea then, love, while I'm here?' he said at last, and gave her a bit of a lopsided smile.

It did the trick because Jade rolled her eyes in a way that reminded the Colonel of a grown-up woman, not his little niece, and then she led the way indoors.

Inside the place was pretty much of a tip but no worse than the Colonel expected. Nothing, really, compared with the places he'd lived in he was that age. She led the way through a back sitting room strewn around with computer parts and computer magazines and into the kitchen where she put the kettle on.

'Nice place,' said the Colonel, feeling more useless than ever. 'You sharing?' He felt pretty sure Jade wasn't a computer boffin.

'Yeah,' she said. 'Digger lives here. It's his place really.'

'He your boyfriend?'

Jade rolled her eyes again. 'Digger? You're joking.'

She made the tea, gave the Colonel a mug and led the way back into the sitting room. She turned the CD player on, shifted a monitor off the sofa, sat down, her knees drawn right up under her chin, and started chewing on her hair.

The Colonel sipped on his tea, started to say something, then found himself distracted by the music, some sort of rap nonsense – kind of thing the Colonel, who was a Springsteen man himself, generally just tuned out – except the fellers rapping all had these full-on Newport accents and were going on about driving round Newport selling draw, and despite himself the Colonel couldn't help laughing.

'What the bloody hell is this?' he asked Jade.

Jade looked up, her hands already engaged in building a spliff. 'GLC,' she said, 'innit.'

The Colonel frowned with incomprehension.

Jade sighed. 'Goldie Lookin Chain. It's a group puts out tunes on the net. All the clarts loves them.'

The Colonel had had enough of this. No way he was going to be drawn into asking what a clart was when it was at home. 'Well,' he said, 'sounds like shit to me anyway.'

Jade rolled her eyes and the Colonel figured he'd started digging a hole so he might as well carry on. 'Look,' he said, 'you want to stop skinning up, and tell me what's going on here, your situation.' He paused, not sure really what he was asking, but no matter, he'd already succeeded in outraging Jade.

'Stop skinning up? You got a nerve. Who was it gave me my first spliff?'

The Colonel winced. 'Yeah, well,' he said, 'I'm not saying you shouldn't smoke draw, I'm just saying there's a time and a place.' Oh yes, like he hadn't dumped his football career in the toilet all those years back after reckoning that the time and the place was in the Cardiff City dressing room, half-time against Wolves.

Maybe Jade knew that story too. Either way, she didn't pay any attention, just carried on rolling, and the Colonel could feel himself about ready to lose his temper, which would screw the whole thing up once and for all, when the doorbell rang. Three short rings, one after the other.

Jade immediately broke out in a big smile. 'That'll be him,' she said, and jumped up to get the door.

The Colonel had a moment to wonder what this bloke would be like. Probably one of those Burberry-clad scallies he'd passed on his way to Pill, with an ancient XR3i parked outside, sound system making the whole street vibrate, about as likely to take responsibility for a kid as get a proper job. The Colonel knew the sort.

Except the bloke walking into the room now with Jade wasn't like that, some dodgy teenager. No, much worse than that. He was a friend of the Colonel's.

'Cyril,' he said, 'thought you were dead.'

'No, bra,' said Cyril, a feller the Colonel knew as a sometime DJ, sometime local councillor, sometime drinking partner and full-time reprobate, 'not dead, just living in the 'Port.'

Cyril laughed but the Colonel didn't join in. He was just trying to work out how the hell he felt about this. Here was Cyril, feller the Colonel had known from time, and couldn't be more than a couple of years younger than him. And here was his niece.

Now in the general course of things, say the Colonel was standing at the bar in the Oak and Cyril comes by and they get to talking and Cyril mentions he's seeing a nineteen-year-old, well, it has to be said most likely thing is the Colonel would buy him a drink, say good for you, mate. And maybe underneath, half of him would be thinking just that, like you lucky bastard, and maybe another half would be thinking isn't there getting to be a bit of an age gap there – like that Steely Dan song 'Hey Nineteen' with the line about she's never heard of Aretha Franklin, all of that. But, yeah, in public the Colonel would have mostly been like good on you, mate.

But not when it was his niece, he wouldn't. She was just a big kid was all. Course that was the problem with these girls nowadays – all getting on the Internet and pretending to be older than they are and running off with Marines. What was wrong with boys their own age? Actually, even as he was thinking this, the Colonel had to acknowledge it had always been that way. Back when he was fourteen, fifteen, did girls look at him twice when there was some older feller got a job and motorbike in the running? No they did not. Still that wasn't the point. Point was, Jade was his niece and it was his job to protect her. From herself if need be, judging by the way she was snogging Cyril right in front of him.

He coughed. Didn't do any good. He coughed again. Cyril broke off the kiss, winked at the Colonel who frowned back at him. Cyril got the message, broke the clinch with Jade.

'How about you get us old timers a cup of tea?' he said, and Jade smiled and trotted obediently into the kitchen.

Cyril waited till she'd gone, then looked at the Colonel quizzically.

'She's my niece,' said the Colonel.

'Ah,' said Cyril, 'I hear you, man. That's cool. I'll look after her. No worries.'

'No worries,' said the Colonel, 'you're joking. She's fucking pregnant. Her mum's doing her nut.'

Cyril looked bewildered. 'She can't be,' he said.

The Colonel waited for him to explain why that might be, then gave him another glare to speed the process up a bit.

'I've had the fucking snip, haven't I? This brer's paid all the child support he's going to, you knows what I'm saying?' His bewilderment turned to something that looked surprisingly like hurt. 'You sure?' he asked the Colonel, his voice lowered.

The Colonel shrugged. 'It's what she told her mum.'

'Fucking Christ,' said Cyril, his mood now heading fast towards anger, and the Colonel readied himself for trouble, but instead Cyril just turned and without another word walked out of the house, slamming the front door behind him.

Jade came out of the kitchen, carrying a tray with three mugs of tea and a plate covered in carefully laid out

Hobnobs. The sight of her pulled at the Colonel's heartstrings. She looked, he thought, like a little girl playing house.

'Where's he gone?' she said.

'Out,' said the Colonel non-committally.

Jade turned on him, furious. 'What did you say to him?'

'Nothing,' said the Colonel, 'just mentioned about you being pregnant.'

Jade looked at him in horror. 'What d'you do that for? I haven't even told him myself. Oh God, he's probably completely freaked out now. Christ, Uncle Ronnie, I thought you were cool.' And with that she slammed the tea tray down and headed off out the door after Cyril.

Oh bollocks, thought the Colonel and stood there paralysed for a moment, feeling idiotically upset at the notion that he'd blown his cool in the eyes of his niece. Then he pulled himself together and headed out the door too.

Outside he couldn't see either of them. He walked past the former tattoo parlour and on to Commercial Street. Still no sign. Which way to go? He decided left towards the docks rather than right towards the town centre. These kinds of situation people mostly head for solitude, not crowds.

He headed down Commercial Street keeping his eyes open, sticking his head into the little storefront pubs that dotted the street, the Top of the Range, the Alexandra and the Welsh Prince, more like bars in Ireland than the gin palaces you tended to get in Cardiff, let alone the new breed of theme bars. No sign of Cyril or Jade in any of them.

In fact, as he walked along, the Colonel was starting to feel sorry for Cyril. He'd really looked hurt when he'd heard Jade was pregnant. Looked like the tired old feller he was and the Colonel could relate to that. For the most part, the Colonel was pretty thankful he was in a solid domestic set-up with Nat – he just wouldn't have the energy to be running round after a nineteen-year-old. Obviously she must have been knocking off someone else on the sly. Some feller a bit closer to her own age, the Colonel rather hoped. Christ, what a mess. Only one thing for it really, he supposed, do what her mum said – have the abortion, put it down to experience. Poor kid.

He came to the end of Commercial Street, still no sign, followed the road round past the church where they had the Pill Historical Exhibition and the old police station and came out by the dock gates. He was about to give up the chase as a bad job when he saw her. She was just off to the left, walking towards the Transporter Bridge.

He called her name. She turned her head, saw him, carried on walking for a few paces as if deliberately ignoring him, then she came to a halt and waited.

Up close he could see she was crying. He opened his arms wide and she let him hug her while she cried.

'Is it 'cause he doesn't want any more kids, Uncle Ronnie?' she said, 'is that it? 'Cause he needn't worry, I'll do all the work, all the looking after the baby. I'll get up in the night and everything. Won't be no trouble.'

Jesus, thought the Colonel, what was it with girls? Why would a girl her age want to throw all her opportunities in life away over some guy like Cyril? Not that he was a bad feller or anything, you wanted a laugh, game of pool, whatever, Cyril was your man, but a father for your kids, well, the Colonel couldn't quite figure it. He was old enough to be her dad, for Christ's sake. Even looked a bit like her dad. Yeah well, maybe that was something to do with it.

'Look,' he said, once she'd stopped crying, 'why don't we have a sit down over the road?' He nodded towards the pub on the corner, feeling like he for one could definitely use a drink.

Jade just shrugged and followed him, then went to the Ladies while the Colonel got the drinks in, pint for himself and a Coke for Jade, seeing as she was pregnant.

He was three-quarters of the way through his pint by the time Jade emerged, a funny sort of smile on her face.

'Uncle Ronnie,' she said, once they were sat in the furthest corner from everyone else. 'I've got my period.'

At first the Colonel didn't know whether to be furious or relieved. In the end he went with relieved. 'You want a vodka in that Coke then?'

'Yeah,' said Jade, 'thanks.'

The Colonel went back to the bar and while he was standing there, waiting for the aged barman to take his eyes off the golf, who should walk into the pub but Cyril. And the Colonel watched as he went over to Jade and he couldn't hear but could imagine the harsh words being said and then he could identify just the moment when

Jade told Cyril that she wasn't pregnant because then Cyril slid in next to her and by the time the Colonel came over with Jade's drink she was all over Cyril and he wasn't complaining either and really they looked so happy he just put the drink down and headed on out into the street, leaving his niece to make her own mistakes.

DERYCK

TEMPERANCE TOWN

Deryck Davies was coming home, the last place on earth
he wanted to be. Call it the docks, call it the bay, call it
bastard Butetown, it was still the same dump he'd
dragged himself out of years ago and now he was being
dragged back in. No doubt some fucking senior brass was
wetting himself over what a good idea it was. Docks-boy
copper due for promotion – don't want him swanning
around Whitchurch or Radyr or anywhere decent people live – nah, send him to Butetown. Be at home there,
won't you, Davies?

Would he hell. Well, he knew what he had to do.
Two years, that's what he had to do. Two years of
keeping his head down and doing the job and then he'd
put in for a transfer somewhere he'd never been, somewhere he'd just be one more copper and not Cyril's boy,
Deryck, joined the police.

He should never have come back to Wales in the first
place, that was the truth of it. Except what could he do,
his mam was sick and who else had she got? And Swansea

had been OK. Fair share of idiots of course in and out the force, but he'd done well. Got his promotion. One thing about Swansea people, they hate Cardiff. One reason he liked being there, he supposed. He hated Cardiff and all.

And here was the turn-off, Cardiff West. And docks. Christ, he could feel his hands sweating on his nice leather steering wheel. Nice leather steering wheel in his nice new car – Volvo he'd bought to cheer himself up when he got the news. Extravagant of course but it wasn't like he had a family or anything – he could afford it. God knows where he'd park it mind, didn't leave a car like that around the docks for long. Or maybe you did, local boys probably too dumb to nick anything isn't a Beemer or a Merc.

He was half tempted to stop at the services, have a coffee, but decided to carry on – no point in delaying the inevitable. Four or five miles down the ring road and he could see the city spread out to the left. Amazing how the stadium dominated everything these days. Couple more miles and he was on the long bridge over the mouth of the Taff, water to the right of him, Asda to the left. And then he was turning off left just before the underpass, coming up for air by Techniquest, one more left turn and there he was, parked outside the Butetown nick. Back home.

Half an hour before Deryck Davies walked through the doors of Butetown nick, and forty minutes before Jimmy Fairfax came out to say hello to him, a girl got off a bus at, where else, the bus station. The girl had black hair scraped back in a ponytail and visible bruising around the left cheekbone of her pretty but sullen face. She was wearing a Nike tracksuit that looked like she'd slept in it and carrying a pink Ellesse backpack.

She stood at the bus stop for a moment, looking around apparently getting her bearings, then headed off towards the Burger King on the corner between the bus station and the train station. In the Burger King she ordered a coffee and took it to a window table where she put her backpack on her knee and went through it briefly, before pulling out a piece of paper which contained an address. She looked at the piece of paper carefully, then returned it to her backpack.

She sat there for a while longer watching the world go by, then finished off her coffee, chucked the paper cup in the bin, then walked towards the Arab-looking bloke by the till.

'Excuse me,' she said, 'do you know where a pub called the Custom House is?'

The bloke looked at her a little askance then said, 'Yeah, it's not far, you just follow the railway like' – his arm pointed out of the Burger King towards the train station – 'till you come to, I think it's the second or third turning on your right, it's called Bute Street. You go under the railway bridge and the pub's on your right.' He lowered his voice, then, 'Bit rough though, love.'

And then he must have taken in the bruising on the woman's cheek, because he quickly turned his gaze away, as if to say none of my business.

'Yeah?' said the woman. 'Thanks for the warning.'

★   ★   ★

Deryck was in the pub with a DC called Jimmy Fairfax
who he half remembered from primary school and he was
pissed off. First off he wasn't much of a drinker, not a
social one anyway, second if he was going to drink he
didn't like pubs, and third if he did have to drink in a pub
he certainly didn't want to be doing it at lunchtime. Feller
like this Jimmy Fairfax, all how ya doing, mate, let's get
them in, larging it up in his off-duty Aquascutum, well, if
he wanted to end up sitting on a reception desk aged fifty
with an Irish tan that was his business.

But first time he showed his face in the nick, what
choice did he have, unless he wanted everyone to take
him for a cunt from the off, and right now, listening to
this Jimmy blundering down memory lane, he wondered
if that wouldn't have been the best option, get it over
with.

'So right,' Jimmy was saying, 'you must remember
Kenny? Kenny Ibadulla?'

Deryck shook his head. He hardly remembered anyone from school in Cardiff.

'No,' he said, 'like I said I was only in secondary for a
year, then we moved, me and my mum.'

'Oh right, yeah well, I suppose,' said Jimmy. 'Still,
thought you might remember Kenny. Anyway you'll be
seeing a fair bit of him now.'

'Yeah?'

'Oh yeah,' said Jimmy, 'regular godfather he is down
here, Kenny, got a couple of clubs, security firm, you
know the sort of deal, and the DS has a right hard-on for
him.'

'Uh huh,' said Deryck, filing that away. One thing he hated in police work was all the stupid little grudges got in the way of doing a proper job. All you needed was some local hard boy and a DS stuck in a pissing contest.

'Yeah well,' said Jimmy, 'just thought I'd give you the heads-up on that. Be honest, it's a pain in the arse. You ask me, all you need to do, place like this, is keep things nice and quiet. No point in stirring up trouble you don't need to.'

Deryck nodded non-committally, stared down into his barely touched pint of lager. He knew what fellers like this Jimmy Fairfax meant when they talked about keeping things quiet – sure, you can keep your pub open all night, long as me and the lads get a free drink, yeah sure, you can sell your drugs, long as you don't sell any to the Lord Mayor's kids, and any time I want a little something for the weekend you sort me out gratis, yeah course you can run a brothel long as the sign out front says Sauna & Massage and long as there's a freebie any time I fancy one. Deryck despised coppers like that.

He looked over at Jimmy's empty glass and stood up.

'You want another one, mate?'

Two hours later Deryck had escaped from the pub, been to see the estate agent and now he was moving his stuff, such as it was, into the flat he was renting in a place called Adventurer's Quay. It was costing him way too much. No doubt he could have found a place in the city for half the money. But if he was going to stick this posting he felt like he had to have a bolthole, a place he could stand to be in. And this was ideal. It was a brand-new identikit upmarket waterfront development. A little soulless maybe, but Deryck didn't mind soulless. In fact he welcomed it. He liked clean and new and shiny. He hated, physically couldn't stand, being in some place that had all the patina and stink and greasy handprints of age and use, lying in a bath that countless others had shed their skin in, cooking on some ancient Belling full of the oven grease of unknowns. Sickening.

The other thing he liked was the view. It was all water, first the bay then the barrage and beyond it the Bristol Channel. It wasn't blue and Mediterranean and beautiful or anything, it was grey and windswept and cold but there was something about open water that spoke to him. Next weekend he would bring his boat down from Swansea, find a berth in the Marina over the other side of the bay. Whenever he was off duty he could be on the water. The thought lifted his spirits immediately and, working with a will, he brought up his bags from the car, put his clothes in the bedroom, set up his micro hi-fi in the kitchen, and put on a Diana Krall CD, a little jazz to listen to while he ironed his shirts for the week.

The woman was sat in the corner of the Custom House over by the door to the lounge. She had a glass of Coke in front of her and a copy of the *Echo* turned to the classifieds. Even in repose it was hard to say how old she was – could have been twenty-five and seen a few things or an unmarked thirty-five. Chances are she was somewhere in the middle.

The regular barmaid, Sue, who was six months pregnant and too knackered to do more than lean on the edge of the bar, could see her eyes moving between the paper and the pub, trying to suss out the scene.

Right now, four o' clock on a Tuesday afternoon, the scene consisted of a couple of girls, Lorraine and her mate, playing pool, another bunch – Scotch Lesley's gang – sat over by the jukebox, getting arseholed as per. There was some old boy from the Valleys with his head in his hands over by the door, pint of Dark half empty in front of him. She was pretty sure he was asleep but she hadn't the energy to go over and give him a dig in the back wake him up. It was the quiet time, really. Another hour or so there'd be half a dozen girls working the six o'clock rush, whipping in and out the pub for drinks and fags, while their pimps sat inside in the warm.

The woman with the *Echo* stirred, folded her paper up, stuck it in her backpack and came up to the bar.

'You need any bar staff?' she asked.

Sue looked at her, half tempted to say sure, love, take my job, please. She felt like a bloody whale already and how she was going to cope with two more months, God only knew. But God also knew she needed the money and this girl should be able to find something – she wasn't bad-looking except for, Christ, a nasty bruise over her left eye. Didn't notice it under the make-up from a distance but up close you couldn't miss it. For an instant she wondered what her story was, then shook the thought away. Everyone in the Custom House had a sad story to tell; why else would they be there? Listen to them all, it'd break your heart.

'Sorry, love,' she said, 'nothing doing here, I'm afraid.'

'Oh,' said the woman, 'right, thanks,' her mouth turning down.

Sue shrugged, not her problem, and the girl started to turn away when a voice said, 'Try the North Star, lovely.'

Sue turned to see who'd spoken. Lorraine, the half-caste Lorraine with the hair, not the other one. 'Yeah, love,' she said, 'North Star needs a new barmaid, heard it last night.'

'Oh yeah?' said Sue, drawn in despite herself. 'What happened to Andrea?'

'Got sent down, didn't she? Cutting that girl outside couple of months ago.'

'Oh yeah,' said Sue and was just about to say to the woman look, that's the kind of place we're talking about here, but before she could say anything the woman just nodded – not smiled or frowned or anything – just nodded and said, 'OK, thanks, where is this place?' and Lorraine told her.

Deryck's second day at work, middle of the afternoon, he had the pleased-to-meet-you get-together with his boss, a DS called McKenzie, and at the end of it McKenzie says, 'First thing you need to do, son, is get the lie of the land. I'll have Jimmy Fairfax give you the guided tour.'

So Deryck says, 'Yes, sir, good idea, sir,' and sure

enough, just on six, couple of hours before Deryck's shift ends, Jimmy Fairfax sticks his head round the side of Deryck's cubicle, rattles his car keys, says, 'Let's get moving then.'

'OK,' says Jimmy, once they're sat in the car. 'Well, I don't have to tell you too much about the city, do I? You're from here and all.'

'Yeah,' says Deryck, 'but I was only a kid and anyway the place has changed.' Which was true enough. In fact Deryck was finding his memories a hindrance rather than a help. There seemed to be roads all over the place where he was pretty sure there didn't used to be roads, and then there was the Stadium in the middle of the city which seemed to have changed the city's centre of balance somehow.

'OK,' said Jimmy, 'fair play, boss. I'll give you the full out-of-towner treatment.'

He drove out of the car park and down Dumballs Road, a nondescript strip of light industry and half-built new blocks of upmarket flats. Which brought them out at the back of the train station. Heading under the railway bridge Jimmy pointed out a club on the right.

'Hippo,' he said, 'popular with the docks boys. Lot of dealers, whatever. Not technically on our patch though so we don't have to worry about that. Still, you need to find someone middle of the night, keep it in mind.'

They were into the town centre then and Jimmy waved a hand at the stadium. 'You been there yet?'

'No,' said Deryck, who had no interest at all in team sports. 'Any good?'

'S'all right,' said Jimmy. 'Does the job, you know. Doesn't have the atmosphere of the old place, not really.'

As Jimmy turned the car round just by the stadium Deryck watched as a girl in her mid-teens, wearing a T-shirt that said 'Nice Melons', leaned over and threw up on the pavement, right outside Yates' Wine Lodge.

Jimmy saw where Deryck was looking and grinned. 'All weekend, boss, it never stops. Worst job in the city cleaning up after them.' He shook his head. 'You know what they used to call this part of town, Del, before they built the old Arms Park on it?'

Deryck shook his head.

'Temperance Town,' said Jimmy. 'Got that one wrong, didn't they?'

'Sure did,' said Deryck and laughed too and the atmosphere in the car eased a little as Jimmy showed him a few more key locations before swinging back towards the bay, heading this time up Bute Street, Butetown's main artery. He slowed as they approached the Custom House pub, then turned right to head down the side of the pub, where three or four girls were standing smoking and waiting for business. A dark girl with her hair in a ponytail caught sight of Jimmy, smiled and flicked him a V sign. Jimmy wound his window down. 'All right, Kell?'

'Jim,' she said, then peered past him at Deryck. 'Who's your mate then?'

'DS Davies,' says Jimmy, then turned round to Deryck. 'Del, this is Kelly, she's a leisure consultant,' and Kelly says, 'Fuck off, Jimmy,' and Jimmy laughs and drives on.

'That's the Custom House beat, Del. Mostly it's quiet enough. Now and again – match days, whatever – there's a bit of aggro. Most of the time though myself and Terry look after it.'

Deryck nodded, figuring he knew exactly what Jimmy meant by looking after a place like that. Taking payoffs from all sides, most likely.

Next ten minutes Jimmy took them round the Butetown Estate, pointing out local landmarks, the mosque, the pub, the shops and the rat runs, stopping every now and then for a quick word with a bunch of Somali guys here, an old lady there. Deryck wasn't sure about this Jimmy, but you had to give him his due, he definitely knew his manor, a real community copper all right. Wasn't the kind of copper he wanted to be himself. Deryck was on the Accelerated Promotion Programme and the sooner he was out of day-to-day contact with the general public the better, far as he was concerned. But still, he could appreciate what Jimmy was doing.

As for Deryck himself, he was doing his best to concentrate on what Jimmy was telling him, but he was finding it hard because he couldn't stop himself from looking. Every time they saw a middle-aged feller walking by he had to check, 'cause he knew, in a small place like this, sooner or later he was going to see him.

Ten years it'd been now since he'd seen his dad and he would have been quite happy to let it run to twenty, thirty, forty in the unlikely event his dad lived that long. Wasn't like he'd ever been any kind of father to Deryck, any kind of husband to Deryck's mum. He'd just been the guy who'd ruined his mother's life and the best thing she ever did was get away from him and his world.

But now Deryck was back in town and sooner or later he was going to run into him. Couldn't help wondering what the old bastard was up to now. No doubt Jimmy would know. That was what he couldn't stand about this place, the sense that everyone knew everyone else's business. Matter of days everyone would have him pegged – Cyril's boy, joined the police. Still, might as well know, forewarned, forearmed, et cetera. He cleared his throat.

'Sounds like a funny question, I know, but is my dad still around?' He wondered for a second if Jimmy would know what the hell he was talking about but sure enough Jimmy smiled at once.

'Cyril? Oh yeah, now and again. Lives over Newport these days, but he's still around. Does a little bit of DJing too Sunday night at the Windsor. They have a little session for the older crowd; your old feller plays the records . . .' Jimmy paused. 'You don't see much of him then?'

'No,' said Deryck.

Jimmy looked as if he was going to say something then but clearly thought better of it and concentrated on the driving, pointing out a few more docks landmarks that Deryck half remembered – the Coal Exchange, the Dowlais – strippers on Wednesday – the Casablanca itself, an old Chapel long since turned into a nightclub, and then, round another couple of corners, almost on the waterfront, another converted chapel –

this one a tiny little place apparently made out of corrugated iron.

'That's the North Star,' said Jimmy. 'Hustlers, queers, sailors and deadbeats.'

'What's your name then, love?' Pat, the landlady of the North Star, asked her new barmaid.

'Lianna,' said the woman.

'Nice,' said Pat, giving Lianna such a frank up-and-down appraisal that she wasn't sure if it was her name or her body Pat was talking about. 'So, you done much bar work?'

'Yeah, well, you know, a bit.'

Pat laughed. 'Well, long as you can add up.' She waved at the array of drinks behind the bar. 'Simple really, there's nothing on draught so you don't have to worry about pulling pints. Cans of beer in the fridge there, spirits up there, mixers underneath. Anyone asks you for a cocktail you tells them to fuck off. All that side of it's easy enough, love, difficult bit is the punters. You know what kind of people comes down here?'

Lianna looked hesitant but nodded. 'I think so.'

Pat looked at her closely. 'You're not on the game, are you, love?'

Lianna didn't say anything, just shook her head.

' 'Cause I don't care if you are or not. But not on my time, all right?'

'I'm not . . .' started Lianna.

Pat shook her head. 'Sorry if I'm insulting you, love, but you're going to get a lot worse than that you start here. First bunch of sailors get in here tonight, been out at sea for a month, they're going to be all over you.'

'I'll be all right,' said Lianna.

Pat smiled at her. 'Well, we'll see, love. Now shift starts at ten so you got couple of hours if you want to go back home for a bit. You live local?'

Lianna looked momentarily panicked. 'No,' she said, 'well, I only just got here. I don't have . . .'

Pat rolled her eyes. 'Oh for Chrissake, love. What are you thinking of? You can't stay in here.' She frowned, thought for a moment. 'C'mon, you need somewhere to stay; we'll go see Mr Singh. He'll have a room for you.'

Jimmy seemed to have come to the end of his grand tour of the manor. He had parked up by the Norwegian Church and the two of them were now standing by the water's edge, looking out at the Bay, Jimmy smoking, Deryck wondering what this was in aid of. Looking out at the Channel he could see a cargo ship approaching.

He pointed at it. 'That one coming in?' he asked, just for something to say.

Jimmy squinted out to sea. In the near dark there was nothing to see but a dark silhouette and some lights. He looked at his watch.

'Dunno,' said Jimmy, 'probably. There's one due in tonight, I think.'

'Yeah?' said Deryck. 'Busy, are they, the docks these days?'

Jimmy shrugged. 'Ticks along, I think. Not like it used to be obviously, but the thing is really I suppose it was a hell of a long time since it did anything more, really. This whole place. Tiger Bay, whatever, way people talk about it now it's like it was something special, but you and me, right, we know it was just the docks.' He flicked his fag over the edge. 'Anyway enough of that. Yeah, there's still a few ships, not much to do with us though, really. Now and then someone's caught nicking stuff out one of the warehouses or whatever but that's about it. Bit of trouble now and again with the sailors, but nothing too tasty, not lately. No,' he said, turning to Deryck, 'what you'll find down here is it's pretty quiet like, and way I see it – don't know about you on your fast track and all – is that it's our job keep it nice and quiet, you know what I mean?'

'Uh huh,' said Deryck, non-committal but with a little bit of edge.

Jimmy caught it, his eyes hardened immediately but he kept a smile on his face. 'Arright, boss,' he said, 'time I took you back to the station.'

It was just past midnight, Lianna had been working for two hours now and she was on her own behind the bar. Andi, she knew he spelt it with an I because he'd told her so second he met her, was over in the corner playing records on the clapped-out sound system, seventies stuff mostly, the beginning of Chaka Khan's 'I'm Every Woman' was just starting up, to cheers from a bunch of drunken hustlers sat right in front of Lianna. Pat the landlady had disappeared off out back on some unspecified errand. And now a short black guy was getting up from the table with the hustlers and walking over to the bar.

'You doing all right, girl?'

'Fine,' said Lianna, not really looking at the guy, her gaze fixed on a bunch of sailors sat round three tables pushed together at the back of the club.

'You need any more stock?'

'I dunno,' said Lianna, her tone lifeless.

'Well,' said the bloke with exaggerated patience, 'why don't you check for us, girl.'

Lianna sighed, looked down below the level of the bar, pushed a couple of beer bottles aside and surveyed a stash of little plastic baggies which Lianna knew to contain eighths of black which she was to sell at £20 each, and a bunch of paper wraps which she understood to contain grams of speed for retail at a very reasonable £10 each. She looked up again.

'I dunno, I got four wraps of speed left – that enough?' her tone still lifeless.

'Yeah, girl,' said the black guy, trying to inject a little life into their exchange, 'you'll be needing re-stocking. Give me the takings so far and I'll be back.'

Lianna didn't say anything, just shrugged, reached down and pulled out from just underneath the till a pile of notes.

'How much you got for me?' said the guy.

Lianna shrugged. 'I dunno, not counting, am I? Hundred maybe, whatever I've sold, innit.'

The guy, whose name was Mikey, shook his head, leaned in close to her. 'Thing about you pretty girls, you don't half have an attitude problem. You going to last round here, you going to have to lighten up. And Mikey Thompson's the feller to help you.' He winked lewdly at Lianna and headed for the exit.

Lianna gave no sign at all she'd heard a word he'd said. Went back to watching the sailors.

Sunday night, end of his first week, Deryck was stood in the window of his clean, empty flat, scanning the horizon hoping for something, anything, to distract him.

The week had gone OK. The other coppers were all right; that's to say they let him be. He knew what they must think: pushy, unfriendly bastard on a fast track, thinks he's better than the rest of us. Fine by him, that's just what he did think. He didn't want to meet their wives, go to their barbeques. Knew what they no doubt whispered – stuck-up twat, thinks he's chocolate, all of that. Water off a duck's back, all of it. The other coppers would soon see he was good at his job, and on the street they'd soon know he was fair, hard but fair. Way his mum had brought him up and there wasn't a damn thing wrong with it.

Weekend – the time he'd been not quite dreading but certainly not looking forward to – had been all right too. Well, Saturday he'd ended up working, which was fine. And Sunday, today, he'd been out on the water, getting his boat sorted out then taking a little trip around the bay. One thing about sailing, you were so caught up in all the physical stuff, you didn't have too much time for introspection.

But now, looking out the window, Norah Jones singing quietly in the background but Deryck not listening, he was feeling the pull all right. He resisted then wavered. No harm in going out for a drink, was there, said the siren voce inside his head. What was the point, he answered himself. He wanted a drink he could just stay in his nice flat, open up one of those nice bottles of wine he had in the kitchen. Not the same though drinking alone, said the siren voice. Natural to want a bit of company, isn't it, and you're a copper you should get to know the neighbourhood. Oh God, if only Jimmy Fairfax hadn't shown him exactly where to go.

First person he noticed after his eyes had adjusted to the darkness inside the North Star was the barmaid. Jet-black hair, white, white face, frail skinny thing, looked weak around the mouth, well, not weak exactly, just not hard like you expected everyone to be in a place like this.

He asked her for a drink. Whisky.

'Single or double?' she asked, her eyes looking down, not catching his.

'Double,' he said and she poured it and took his money, looking like she was concentrating all the time, remembering how to do it right. Again, not what you expected in a place like this.

He looked around, confirming to himself exactly what kind of place this was.

There was a dance floor at one end with a tiny DJ set-up to one side, some rat-faced gayboy leaning over it, selecting the next record. Two girls were dancing together to the current one, Michael Jackson's 'Don't Stop Till You Get Enough', first record Deryck had ever bought as it went, and those strings still thrilled him, but now it was just a beat for two drunken hookers – a fat blonde one and a skinny one whose hair was just about giving up on the remnants of its blonde dye-job – to fall around to. He eyed the fat one. She might do.

Opposite the bar there was a bunch of tables, more hookers, some black guys, probably pimps or dealers or both, one of them, a little guy with one of those smiley faces you didn't trust an inch, was giving him a bit of a look. Well, let him look – probably thought Deryck was about to move in on their territory. Well, he would do that all right in his own good time, but not the way they were thinking. Bunch of sailors over in the corner, looked eastern European, one of them calling out to the girls on the dance floor. Let him and all, Deryck wasn't in a hurry.

He turned back to the barmaid. 'You been here long?' he asked.

She half turned towards him, had caught his voice, not what he said. He motioned her closer and repeated himself.

'No,' she said, 'not long,' dropping her eyes down again and quickly turning as if someone had called to her from further down the bar. No one had though. Deryck wondered what she was so nervous about. And while he was wondering he stared at her long white neck, thinking other things, his tongue running along his teeth, and then his teeth suddenly clamping down on it, hard.

He finished his whisky and ordered another one, got the same eyes looking anywhere but at him treatment. He kept his profile low, just one more solitary drinker, no one to worry about. He watched the barmaid serve other people, saw she was no easier with them. The sailors liked her, of course, liked anything with tits after God knows how long on the water. The hookers were friendly enough but the girl barely responded, then one of the hookers whispered something in her ear while she was ordering and quite clearly Deryck saw the barmaid reach under the counter and pick something up and palm it over to the hooker.

Oh right, that was interesting. He looked round behind him. Had anyone seen him notice? He didn't think so. He leaned back on his stool, savoured the feeling of power that came with that kind of knowledge, knowledge that could make a person do what you want. The best, the very best thing about being a copper. Felt it right there.

He would bide his time though, no need to rush. Not with that one. That was one to savour. For tonight he would settle for . . . would settle for the big blonde heading out of the club now.

He finished his drink, followed the blonde outside.

'You working, love?'

She looked at him, obviously didn't mind what she saw.

'Yeah, love,' her voice slurring, 'all right, long as you don't take too long. I knows what you boys are like.'

'You boys', that was good, that gave Deryck the edge

he wanted when, five minutes later in a newish but already dilapidated council flat, he slammed into her again and again, his hands round her front, grabbing her tits hard then round her white milky throat, oblivious to the sounds she was making, till he'd got to where he had to be and it left him and he could let her flop down beneath him and she started to swear at him, telling him she'd call the cops, till he pulled out the twenties and kept going till he came to a hundred quid and then her face changed, and they both relaxed into the familiar still awful knowledge of how little people cost.

Later he was back in the flat listening to Joni Mitchell, a bottle of wine already empty by his side, tears rolling down his face. Later still he woke in the night, horrified by his dreams.

In work, the boss had a job for him.

'Long-term investigation,' he said. 'Raj Impex — little import—export firm right there by the Queen Vic Dock. Information received suggests they've been smuggling all sorts. Never managed to firm it up though. Like you to look it over, recommend a course of action.'

Deryck nodded, took the file away. Like the boss said, allegations, no hard evidence. Couple of spot checks hadn't shown anything dodgy up but they wouldn't really, less you got very lucky indeed. Need a full-scale raid to do that and that cost money. Was it likely they were dodgy? Certainly possible: word was that there was a fair deal of coke being moved through Cardiff, coming in from Trinidad. Raj Impex didn't deal with any ships travelling to the West Indies though, far as Deryck could see. Most of their trade seemed to be with the Middle East – Cyprus, Istanbul, somewhere called Batumi in Georgia which, with the aid of an atlas, he located on the Black Sea. Wasn't likely to be cocaine, coming from that part of the world, could be dope, could be, yeah very much could be, smack, now the Afghans were back in business.

If that was it though, why didn't these so-called informants say so instead of these vague little warnings – 'RAJ IMPEX ARE SMUGGLERS' printed on a blank postcard. Crap really, and tempting just to tell the chief forget it, but Deryck wasn't that kind of cop and frankly he was bored. For an inner-city community Butetown was pretty bloody quiet and anyway practically whatever went on, it would turn out that Jimmy Fairfax or one of his mates needed to handle that one personally. Well, Deryck felt like it was about time he handled something personally.

He decided to walk round there, get a sense of how the land lay. Walked down James Street, saw the Casa B off to his left, then the North Star off to his right. He hadn't been back there again, knew it would be madness to go there again; just a matter of time till someone clocked him for a copper.

Past the lights and the illuminated bulk of the UCI and he was through the dock gates and into the other Cardiff Bay, the working bay. He showed his warrant card to the feller on the gate, who started to insist that Deryck wore a hardhat on the dock till Deryck gave him a bit of a look, at which point he shrugged and muttered the directions to Raj Impex.

Deryck found it easily enough, an anonymous two-storey red-brick building, offices at the front, warehouse in back. He peered through the front door at the reception area: no one behind the desk. He decided against going in, instead walked round the side to have a look at the warehouse. Nothing much doing, empty loading bays, a couple of cars parked, barely a sign of life. He turned round, scanned the dock, only one ship in the whole place. God knows why they bothered with all the security on the port gates, the place was obviously dying on its feet.

Just then a car drove past him, very nice top-of-the-range Merc, pulled in next to the other two cars. Feller got out, fortyish white bloke with gelled hair and a suit a little sharper than the average, bit of a player. He set the alarm without looking back at the car, unlocked the back door and went in. Well, thought Deryck, looked like someone was making money at Raj Impex.

He surveyed the dock again, still empty. He closed his eyes trying to remember how it was when he was a kid. Nothing came. Finally he squeezed out a memory of playing with a gang of kids beside a stretch of water somewhere, throwing stones on the water, himself keeping well away from the edge. Terrified of water, he was then. Wonder when that had changed. Anyway, question was, were the docks busier then? Maybe. He remembered bridges, traffic, noise, but only on the edge of things. The docks themselves – the only memories he could conjure were of these great quiet places, kids and stones and weeds and water. No doubt in his dad's time it had been different but all Deryck remembered was dereliction.

He was heading back to the station now, out of the dock gates. Looking round he sought to capture the geography of the old docks, couldn't do it, the UCI and the council offices and the new roads had obliterated, overwritten his memory. And good riddance, frankly.

Crossing the road at the lights he saw her coming out of the Spar. Her, the barmaid from the North Star. She turned, started to walk west down James Street, and as he crossed the road he found himself walking almost in step with her. He didn't expect her to recognise him but she did.

'Oh, hiya,' she said, frowning slightly like she knew she recognised him but not from where.

'All right,' said Deryck and was going to leave it at that, pick up the pace, leave her behind, but something in her eyes stopped him. 'I was in the club the other night,' he said, then added, 'case you were wondering why you recognised me.'

'Oh,' she said, a little half-laugh, 'yes, well, sorry to bother you.'

'No,' said Deryck, 'no bother.'

Which seemed to end the conversation, leaving them walking along awkwardly in sync, the barmaid a couple of paces in front of Deryck. In the daylight he could see she was a slim dark woman, hair in a rough ponytail, clothes from the cheap end of the high street or Splott

Market, ordinary as anything really, you saw girls like this every day, hundreds of them pretty enough when they were young, washed out rags at thirty and this one couldn't be far off thirty, even though there was something almost childish about her features.

Bound to have some dodgy boyfriend sitting at home waiting to smack her around if she got the numbers wrong on his lottery ticket. Deryck knew the type all right, except, except with this one, even from two paces behind and at an angle from which you could see little more than the back of her head, she still radiated a palpable sadness, an absolutely desperate sadness. And something in Deryck responded to that.

What it was though that responded in him was not something he was proud of and in the daylight hours at least it was a call, a hunger, he could ignore, so he crossed the road heading for his nice clean flat without saying another word.

Back at the flat he pored over sailing charts, checked weather forecasts, made plans for his Sunday sail, a trip around Flatholm with an option to round Steepholm as well, if all went to plan. He cooked some noodles and Chinese vegetables, he listened to Diana Krall again, Live at the Olympia. God, there was something almost inhuman in that woman's control, a glimpse of the sublime or the robotic maybe, he wasn't quite sure which, or whether there was a difference either. He slept badly.

In work he did some more research, first on the

Internet where he ran the name Raj Impex through a search engine and came up with nothing much more than he already knew, and then in the canteen where he ran into Jimmy Fairfax.

'Raj Impex,' said Jimmy with a laugh. 'Boss still going on about that? You ask me, he's just pissed off 'cause John Spiller's making more money than he is, rolls up to the golf club in the old 7 series, boss gets a bit green-eyed like.'

'Yeah,' says Deryck, 'I was wondering about that. Seemed like a nice motor for a feller with a little business doesn't look like it's worth shit.'

Jimmy shrugged. 'Lot of people got nice motors, Del boy, don't earn a fortune. Look at me, got the old Beemer in the car park there. Look at you, come to that, that Swedish piece of shit you drive, got to cost a few quid. Don't mean we're bent, just a question of priorities, innit, fronting it up.'

Deryck frowned. 'Yeah maybe, but what do they actually trade in?'

'Crap,' said Jimmy. 'Rugs, lot of rugs – Indian bloke over City Road got a carpet warehouse orders them in, and furniture, ugliest furniture you ever saw in your life and all, looks like stuff you'd stick in the haunted house in *Scooby Doo*, place over Cowbridge Road, by Victoria Park there, got a bloody shedload of it. Those are the main things, plus like fabric and bits and pieces, special orders. They're just middle men really, ship the stuff in, take a percentage.'

'Christ,' says Deryck, 'you know a lot about it.'

'Yeah, boss had me on them last year, waste of time, I can tell you. Well, it's what I told him and all, but I suppose you being the new boy and that he thought he'd stick you back on it. Tell you what I would do – go see the carpet man, go see the furniture feller, tell the boss it's all kosher and would he mind stopping pulling your chain.'

'Right,' said Deryck, 'thanks,' as Jimmy headed back upstairs, whistling.

He was still thinking on what Jimmy had said, wondering if this was just some bloody tiff from the Masonic Lodge or the Rhondda Riviera overspilling on to his desk, when a report of a stabbing over Grangetown came in and he was called on to do some regular police work for the rest of the day.

A suicide, a spate of muggings and an off-licence burglary kept him busy for the next couple of days and he had almost forgotten about Raj Impex till Friday afternoon the boss came by, handed him a white card, said, 'Here you go, we've got another one.'

It was another card like the 'RAJ IMPEX ARE SMUGGLERS' one except this time the message read 'VAL DENNISON OF RAJ IMPEX IS A SMUGGLER AND A DEALER'.

Deryck looked at it. Wasn't much to say really. Whoever had written the card had certainly mastered the art of getting the message across.

'You heard of her, boss?'

McKenzie looked at him, puzzled. Deryck fought back the urge to ask what part of 'VAL DENNISON

IS A SMUGGLER' his boss didn't understand. 'Val Dennison, sir,' he said. 'You heard of her?'

'Oh,' said McKenzie, 'threw me there, Deryck. It's a bloke – he's a bloke. Val Dennison. Valentine, I suppose. He's John Spiller's partner. Travels a lot, I think. Why don't you see what you can dig up?' And with that headed back to his office, leaving Deryck with the piece of card in his hand.

Deryck sat back, thought about it. Then picked up the phone, called Raj Impex's number.

Got hold of a receptionist with a slight Valleys accent said Mr Dennison was out of the office till the eighteenth, ten days' time. Deryck asked if there was any way he could get hold of him and the receptionist hummed and hedged then said Deryck could leave a message but she wasn't sure when he'd get it because he was at sea at the moment.

Deryck said thanks, put the phone down and pondered some more, then went to look for Jimmy, see what he had to say. No sign of Jimmy though or any of his mates. A WPC came over, said Friday afternoon Jimmy and the boys will be in the pub, won't they, and Deryck said thanks and finished off his paperwork and headed home, figuring that if this Dennison was at sea for another ten days he had plenty of time.

After work Deryck went round to the Marina, worked on his boat for while till the light failed. Feller he was talking to, had a Wayfarer in the next berth, invited him for a pint up at the Yacht Club so Deryck said yeah, why not.

Little bit of a surprise when he walked in there, of course, boat clubs are pretty much of a middle-class preserve, but it wasn't anything new or even a problem, you just got people being a little bit over-polite and a bit too thrilled to hear about his boat like he was a talking dog or something.

Anyway the feller, Pete, was fine and Deryck loved talking sailing, so he stayed for a couple and then the club secretary came over tried to persuade him to join, just dying to show what a progressive sort of a place it was, so he filled out the forms and one way or another it was half-nine before he got back to the flat and realised he was hungry and the cupboard was bare.

So it was in search of food that he headed back out, except the Spar was already closed, and the prospect of sitting in one of the flash new restaurants on his own didn't appeal, which left a place called Bab's Bistro, a caff that stayed open all night more or less and while, by and large, he liked to eat healthy, the beer was telling him that some kind of grease and starch combo would be more than acceptable, and in he went and there, sat alone at a table on the right, was the girl from the North Star. And before he knew what he was doing he'd said you mind and she'd given her head a little shake like go ahead and he'd sat down and he'd ordered a steak-and-kidney pie, chips and peas and the girl had said her name was Lianna and she smoked and drank coffee and watched him eat and checked her watch and neither of them said much, but with this weird sort of intimacy a bit like some old couple who've got nothing left to say to each other, not two people who've hardly ever said a word. And finally she said she had to get going over to the club and why didn't he come over later and he said maybe but he knew he would be there for sure 'cause much as ate he was still hungry.

He waited for a while, walked around the bay staring out at the darkness over the water, and then he stopped fooling himself and went into the North Star and almost had a fit when he saw Lianna straight away behind the bar talking to the blonde whore from the other night. And then both of them noticed him and the blonde put her head close to Lianna and started talking animatedly in her ear and Deryck didn't need to be a mind-reader to figure out what she was saying, and if he hadn't had the hunger so badly he would have turned and walked out then and there.

Instead he headed on into the club, surveyed the place carefully for any sign of his fellow officers taking in a bit of r&r, but thankfully there was no sign either that anyone had made him for a copper yet. So he walked over to the far end of the bar where an older woman was holding court and he ordered his whisky and turned round to look around the club looking everywhere but at Lianna, and obviously there was a ship in dock because there was a bunch of sailors sitting at the tables and there were hookers on the dance floor and dealers in the shadows and he really had to get out of this place quickly – it was crazy being here, God knows what excuse he'd come up with except, even as he thought that, he found his excuse.

He was investigating Raj Impex, that's what he'd say, looking for background-informers, whatever, and yeah, that might fly but even so he didn't want to hang around, he just needed to find a girl and go, places like this made his flesh creep, and he was just trying to choose between a skinny little blonde in her early twenties and an older, bigger woman with loads of dark hair and neither of them being quite right so he turned back to the bar to get another whisky and there she was, Lianna, and he was thrown utterly for a second and before he could say anything she spoke not looking at him, her eyes in fact looking directly down at the floor, and her voice very quiet.

'Mel told me what you like,' he thought she said, but could hardly credit it.

'Oh,' he said carefully.

'Yeah,' said Lianna, still looking at the floor, 'that's what I like too.'

Jesus fucking Christ, thought Deryck. 'Uh huh,' he said carefully, not trusting himself to say anything more.

'I finish at three, that too late for you?'

'No,' said Deryck carefully, 'that's not too late, not at all.'

He didn't know, thinking about it, if he'd like it, her wanting it too. Somewhere in his dark heart he thought, he feared, what got him off was them not liking it.

And it was awkward of course, walking back with her to the awful depressing room she rented over a kebab shop and the two of them standing there in the room and

none of the ghastly ease of the straightforward commercial transaction to get them through the next stage, but
no possibility either of just acting like an ordinary first-
date couple – too many cards on the table for that – and
he just stood there like a spare part till thank God she
took the initiative. Even though it was her who was
meant to be the passive one it was her who said, 'Well,
come on then, Mr Copper, you going to do me?' And he
went, 'You what?' like not believing what he heard, but
still instantly angry.

'You heard,' she said, 'you're a copper; that's what the
girls tell me.'

Christ, he thought with one part of his brain, so much
for keeping a low profile, should have known there was
no chance of that in an inbred shithole like this. But just
at that moment the other part of his brain was operating
his mouth.

'What the fuck's it to you?' he said. 'You just get your
fucking clothes off.'

And suddenly they were away at the races. Ugly
words coming out of both their mouths: cunt, copper,
whore, bastard, bitch, fuck you, hurt me, harder,
harder, harder, till at last it was over and as Deryck's
sight and hearing and awareness of the world outside
his lust returned he could already see the bruises
blooming around her neck and in seconds he was
dressed and in minutes back in his own flat, yes, clean
nice flat, and washing and washing till there was no
blood, no marks left on him, just terrified exultant
electrical impulses zapping around his brain threatening

to short-circuit, and he staggered to bed, sure he would never sleep, and must have passed out within seconds of head hitting pillow, sleeping the deepest, most blameless eight hours he'd had in years.

Later in the day though, sailing aimlessly around the Marina, the calmness left him. First he felt the dimmest pangs of the hunger, which was a bad sign. Normally it was a week at least before it came back. This time, though, he found himself contemplating going back to the North Star that night. What the fuck was he thinking of? For one if he kept on seeing this Lianna – this hardly more than a whore barmaid – people would find out and his reputation would be shot.

Two, he was scared. Scared of what might happen he went with her again. How low could he go, he didn't want to know, didn't want to discover what depths he could sink to. He tried to lose himself in the ropes and sails but it was hard and later it took half a bottle of brandy before he passed once more through sleep's dark and silent gate.

Sunday he'd planned to touch up the paintwork on the boat but the weather frustrated his plans, sleeting rain from the moment he woke up, the kind of rain you just knew was settled in for the day. He still needed something to take his mind off things, though. So, his head throbbing from the brandy, he headed into work, thought he'd take the time to sort through some paperwork.

Lunchtime and the fourth person had just taken the piss out of him for coming in on his day off and he was just thinking of going round the pub watch the football when he found himself staring at the latest Raj Impex note, the 'VAL DENNISON IS A SMUGGLER AND A DEALER' one. And just by way of filling in the time he decided to do a little more research. He went through the files, found an address for this Val Dennison, somewhere over in Sully, and decided to have a look, see what kind of style this Dennison lived in, when he wasn't at sea.

He took the Volvo out of the car park, drove west over the bay, then cut through the Edwardian torpor of Penarth and along the coast road past Lavernock Point and the signs advertising something called the Cosmeston Medieval Village before arriving in Sully, a little seaside town that looked to have strayed from the South Coast, a Bournemouth suburb perhaps.

The Dennison residence proved to be a substantial villa overlooking the Bristol Channel, currently barely visible through the endless rain. As a sailor Deryck approved of it thoroughly, as a copper he figured it was for one thing expensive and for a second thing the kind of place you'd expect to find a conservative middle-aged-to-elderly couple living, the kind of place people move when their kids leave home.

The kind of place senior coppers lived, was the thought that buzzed through his brain then, the kind of place McKenzie would live. It was hardly your regular drug-dealer hangout though. Nothing flash or new about this place. The only feature that seemed to differentiate it from any of its neighbours was a series of extraordinarily ugly garden sculptures in pink marble. No, if he was a dealer, this Dennison, he had to be a long way up the food chain. No way was this the kind of place you could have people calling in day and night, anything like that, and Deryck would bet the neighbours would be taking an interest.

Just like they were doing now, in fact. Next door's garden suddenly acquired a regulation late-middle-aged, winter-tanned male occupant pretending to be taking an interest in his flowerbeds, like it wasn't pissing down and he hadn't been dozing in front of the *Antiques Roadshow* till he saw Deryck get out of his car.

'Looking for Mr Dennison?'

Deryck gave a non-committal grunt, and turned his eyes away from Dennison's garden grotesques.

'He's away at the moment, I believe. Travels abroad a lot.'

'Hmm,' said Deryck.

'Shall I tell him you called, Mr . . .'

Deryck looked at the feller, half tempted to tell him to mind his own business, then decided to give the old boy a thrill, and reached into his pocket, pulled out his warrant card.

'Oh,' said the feller. 'It's about the wife, is it?'

Deryck grunted again, wondering what he was talking about.

'Tragic,' says the bloke, 'tragic. You don't think there was anything funny about it, do you?' His tongue practically hanging out in anticipation of some scandalous revelation.

Deryck just busked it, said no actually, he was looking at an apparently unrelated matter involving Mr Dennison but . . . and the feller reckoned that a nod was as good as a wink and launched into an extensive character assassination of Mr Dennison, while suggesting that the late Mrs Dennison, Julie, should be neck and neck with Mother Teresa in the race for canonisation.

Back in the office he pulled out the files on Julie Dennison. Well, he thought then, no wonder the neighbours were interested. Regular Barrymore job, by the looks of it. Drowned in the swimming pool, traces of alcohol, cocaine, fluoxetine and chicken, according to the report. Husband, Mr Valentine Dennison, found her when he returned home at 2 a.m. Oh aye? Said she'd been depressed – hence the fluoxetine. And. And nothing. Apparently that was good enough for all concerned.

Deryck shrugged. He wasn't particularly surprised. Life is not a detective show – people die all the time in ways that if you were watching *Inspector Morse* you'd just know were suspicious. In real life people fall off bridges, overdose on drugs, even though their family swears blind they never touch them, and yes, they drown in swimming pools. They drown in the sea, drown in the bath, for that matter. But throw in the suggestion that the husband might not be the solid citizen he'd obviously passed for, well, that changed matters all right.

He checked the name of the investigating officer, feller named Andrews over in Barry. He'd give him a call, see if there was any more to the story than went into the report. Feller probably wouldn't appreciate it. Enough work to do without some bastard going through your old cases, which would waste your time for definite and quite possibly leave you looking like a total twat in the unlikely event he did turn something up. But well, Deryck could handle that. He didn't take the job because he wanted people to like him.

DC Andrews wasn't there though, mysteriously having something better to do on a Sunday afternoon. So Deryck pottered and tidied and pondered and, walking back to his flat, came up with an idea. What he needed was some inside information on this Raj Impex outfit, and who better to get that from than the sailors they use, and where better to get hold of them than The North Star, and who better to catch them talking unguarded than the barmaid?

Who was he kidding? It wasn't a plan. Well, it was a plan, but he was clear-sighted enough to know that it had only one real object and that was to make him feel better about what he was going to do that night. See her again.

This time he brought a rope. This time was even better, even worse. He used the plan to fill in the time afterwards. Better than running away like he did before. He started talking as he freed her wrists.

'I need you to do something for me,' he said.

'Thought I already did,' she said, coming out of subservient mode quicker than he would have liked. He kept his tone cold, kept his eyes away from the bruises on her neck. The marks of his thumbs on her windpipe, new bruises blooming on the old.

'You get a lot of sailors in the club.'

'Yeah,' she said, 'you noticed.'

'You ever heard of a company called Raj Impex?'

'Dunno,' she said, 'maybe,' but there was something in her eyes, he was sure of it, some flicker of recognition.

'Yeah well,' he said, 'import—export company, offices on the dock. You ask about, you talk to the sailors, you hear anything you tell me.'

'Like what?' she said. 'You looking for a new job?'

'Shut it. They're under investigation, all you need to know.'

She was looking at him now, her expression bewildered, well, not bewildered exactly more 'What is he on?' to be honest. What was he on? He didn't know himself really, but his mouth just blundered on regardless.

'Two names to look out for – John Spiller, he's the boss man, or Val Dennison, specially that one Val Dennison.'

Definitely something in her face at the mention of that name. Definitely. Maybe she did hear things after all. Whatever – time to go. He stood up, started dressing. 'Right,' he said then and was about to add something – 'Got to go' or 'Let me know what you hear', something to make him sound like an in-control copper, not a sad, lonely man who only seemed to come fully alive to himself when he had his hands around her neck – when she interrupted him.

In a quiet voice, different to the one he'd heard her use so far, she said, 'Can I trust you?'

'Yes,' he said, 'of course.'

'You're not . . .' She started to say something then thought better of it. 'No, fuck it.'

'Look,' he said then, 'I don't know what you've heard about me, but I'll bet you one thing you never heard is I was anything but a straight copper. You tell me something, you can trust me.'

She looked up at him, her hand unconsciously rubbing her neck, then a slight smile as she gave it up. 'Look, I do know Val Dennison.'

And then her expression changed again, the smile fled and her face just crumpled into tears.

Deryck stared at her, completely thrown by this new weakness in her. It didn't make sense maybe to see her as strong – the way she submitted to him – but there was a real steely kind of strength in the way she didn't cry out when he hurt her, the way she willed him on to constrict the breath out of her, to push it all the way to the edge, this sense that she was happy with getting what she wanted, not like him who was tormented by it. And never a hint of tears, no matter what he said or did. But now just the mention of this Dennison's name and she came apart.

He didn't say anything, just waited for her to pull herself together, which she did with one great sob and a long exhale of breath and a wiping of the tears from her face.

'I can't tell you why,' she said then, 'but I'll help you all right. If you're going after that bastard then I'll help you.'

Deryck didn't reply for a while, just stared at her trying to compute what she'd just said, feeling almost vertiginous as if the world was spinning, thrown off its axis by someone stepping out of the role they were meant to be playing. Basically he felt out of control and that was the thing he hated. Didn't need a shrink to tell him that, he knew it perfectly well himself – he craved control to an unreasonable, impossible degree. That's why he was a copper, for Christ's sake.

So he put his jacket on, willed himself into professional mode – repeat after me, she's a witness, you're a copper, that's all you need to know – and said, 'Thanks, you do that then. Ask around and I'll be in touch,' and with that he was out of there and back on the street, gulping for fresh air.

Monday morning, Deryck braced Jimmy Fairfax in the canteen, asked him what he knew about Val Dennison.

'Feller whose wife drowned,' said Jimmy, sounding cheery as ever but his eyes flickering.

'Yeah,' said Deryck, 'works for Raj Impex. That one.'

'Yeah,' said Jimmy. 'So what about him?'

'This business with his wife drowning. You hear there was anything dodgy about it?'

Jimmy shrugged. 'Not my patch, Del boy – Barry boys

144

handled it. All I know was what I read in the *Echo*. They gave it a bit of play, cashing in on the Barrymore angle, but sounded like bollocks to me, Del. Bored housewife has a few vodkas too many, passes out in the pool. Why? You heard anything different?'

'No,' said Deryck, 'not really. I just heard a rumour this Dennison is dodgy.'

Jimmy shook his head. 'Boss is really jerking your chain on this one, isn't he? You seen Val yet?'

'No,' said Deryck, 'no cause yet. Anyway he's at sea, not back for another week or so.'

'Oh,' said Jimmy ruminatively. 'On the *Feroza*, with another load of dodgy furniture. You been over the warehouse?'

'Not yet.'

'Well, boss has got you on this full-time – you might as well. Pick up a couple of Clarksies pies on the way back for us and all.'

Deryck laughed, headed back up to his desk. Spent an hour writing up a b & e in Grangetown for Sunday night, then decided to do as Jimmy said, head over Cowbridge Road, have a look at the furniture warehouse.

The warehouse was right at the end of Cowbridge Road East, a lively two-mile stretch of curry houses, video stores and pound shops that perennially clung on the furthest edge of respectability. From the outside the place looked ordinary enough, a low, stone-built warehouse with a sign outside saying 'Canton Collectibles – Furniture from the Orient'.

Inside it seemed huge, partly because the lighting was on the dark side of dim and partly because it was completely cluttered with stuff. You stepped round a row of massive mock-Egyptian garden statues and found yourself confronted by a row of Chinese-ish bedsteads. It was, as Jimmy had said, uncannily reminiscent of the props warehouse for *Scooby Doo*, except this stuff was real and the spookiness was enhanced by the fact the place seemed to be completely deserted.

The silence became steadily more oppressive as Deryck worked his way past hideous fireplaces and uglier yet Japanese-esque room-dividers. He was about to call out in the hope of flushing out some sign of life when he noticed a set of tables in what looked to Deryck's untutored eye like one of those hardwoods that you're not meant to make things out of these days. Could that be the scam – mahogany runners? He rather doubted it but he was bending down to examine them more carefully when he heard a quiet cough behind him.

Deryck turned round to see a middle-aged, Middle Eastern-looking feller in a dark suit standing behind him.

'Can I help you, sir?' Feller's accent was hard to place, something non-European overlaid with a harsh but oddly reassuring veneer of Cardiff.

'Looking for the boss,' said Deryck, straightening up and pulling out his warrant card. Taking control.

'At your service,' said the bloke, raising his eyebrows. 'You want a discount?' A short, humourless laugh. 'Or you got more questions?'

'More questions?' said Deryck, taking his turn with the eyebrow-raising thing.

'Yes, yes,' said the bloke, waving his hand dismissively. 'Last year you fellers were all over me. So discount or questions?'

'Questions,' said Deryck, feeling the control slip away.

'Fine,' said the bloke, sticking out his hand then. 'My name is Ismail. Come into my office, boss, we shall have tea.'

The tea was peppermint-flavoured and Deryck liked it, the way it felt clean on the palate. Made a note to himself to get some. He asked the feller, Ismail, about Raj Impex. Ismail shrugged and sighed and said he'd tell Deryck what he told the other copper. They were middle men, they got the furniture shipped over from Armenia, from Georgia, from Turkey, from India, from wherever. Import—export furniture, that's all. He stopped just short of asking what the hell Deryck's problem was with that, and instead threatened to empty out drawers full of paperwork for Deryck to inspect.

Deryck waved it away, changed tack slightly. 'Who do you deal with at Raj Impex then? Val Dennison?'

Ismail's eyes flickered at that, Deryck was sure. He was getting the feeling that Val Dennison was one of those names no one wanted to hear.

'No,' he said firmly. 'I do all the business with Mr John Spiller.'

'But you know Dennison?'

'No,' said Ismail, 'I don't think I've heard the name. He works for Raj, does he?'

'Yes,' said Deryck, 'that's right,' and closed up his notebook, hoping he sounded purposeful, actually feeling acutely aware that he was blundering about in the dark here, but still nagged by a sense that something was very wrong about this place. For starters it was completely deserted.

'Always this busy, are you?' he said, standing up.

Ismail shrugged, 'It's special orders mostly, not passing trade. For the connoisseur, this stuff,' he said, throwing his arm out towards a family of garden sculptures that looked oddly familiar to Deryck.

It was only as he was getting into the car that he realised why they were familiar: they were the twins of the ones he'd seen in Val Dennison's garden.

Back in work, Deryck spent the rest of the day trying to sort out the provenance of a couple of burnt-out cars parked by the old Hamadryad Hospital, and doing his best to prevent war from breaking out between a couple of shopkeepers over which one was allowed to sell newspapers and which one milk.

Then, around four, he got a call from the estate agents selling his mum's house. Said they'd had an enquiry and could Deryck please get all his mum's crap out of there. Oh well, they didn't say crap but that was what they meant – because it was proving a bit hard to shift it with all that *stuff* in there.

Yeah, well, Deryck could see that. Unless some fellow Jehovah's Witnesses showed up, in which case they would feel right at home. Yeah, he said, checking his shift rota as he talked, he'd be over to clean it out tomorrow morning.

He spent the evening quietly in the flat, cooked himself a Thai curry, paying obsessive attention to the recipe to make sure it took him all evening, listening to Diana Krall Live in Paris, and steeling himself for the morning's ordeal.

In the night he dreamed about Lianna and then about his mother, or was it the same dream? When he woke he wasn't sure when he stopped dreaming about one, started dreaming about the other, and he didn't have to be Sigmund Freud to know he had issues there. He knew that all right; what he didn't know was whether he could face them.

In the morning, driving out to his mother's place, home, as he still thought of it, taking the M4 west towards Swansea, he tried to listen to the Diana Krall, went straight to the Joni Mitchell song that was going round in his head, 'I could drink a case of you and I would I would still be on my feet,' the one where Ms Krall suddenly cuts loose. And then he couldn't stand to listen to music any longer, gave his brain too much opportunity to drift off to think about what he was doing, so he switched to Five Live and listened to Nicky Campbell patronise callers and guests alike as they debated the decline of the educational system.

Even that failed once he saw the dreaming spires of the Bridgend Outlet Shopping Village loom up. He was getting close. A couple more miles, just past the Pile turn-off, and you could see the sea. And then there it was, nestling alongside the Bristol Channel like an alligator by the bayou, the terrible beauty of Port Talbot – not so much a town as a gas works, a steel works and their attendant dormitories, oh and as if by way of a joke, a beach. It was where Deryck's mum had grown up and it was where she'd fled when she left Cyril.

He eased the Volvo off the motorway and without conscious thought threaded his way to his mum's home on a street virtually underneath the motorway. Lovely and quiet it had been, his mum never tired of telling him, before they built that thing, but it had been there since before Deryck was born and the balance of his childhood had been spent looking out over a river of traffic towards an inferno of heavy industry, and beyond that the cool blue of the sea.

He sat outside in the car for what felt like hours and must have been five minutes at least before he willed himself to go in. It was the first time he'd been back since the funeral six weeks before. There'd been a brief wake after the crem, the ladies from the Kingdom Hall had made tea and sandwiches and talked about what a good woman she'd been, and Deryck had stood there frozen and waited for them to go, and afterwards he'd gone to a brothel in Briton Ferry and found a girl there and taken her to the Marriott on the Marina and, and done stuff.

He got out of the car, opened the door and bent to pick up the mound of junk mail. Busied himself with checking there wasn't anything important mixed up in it all, then finally let his eyes start to look round to take in the cross on the wall, the religious paintings, postcards, statuettes, the boxes he'd filled in those unreal, don't call them dead days between heart cease in the hospice and the burning at the crem.

The boxes in the kitchen were safe enough, the pots and pans and five bloody colanders held little threat. The front room too was safe territory: the best furniture and boxes of unused ancient china. The living room was worse – here you could still see the shape of her in her favourite chair, though the brand-new telly had been a surprise. In here were the boxes of unsold *Watchtowers* removed from their shameful hiding places in cupboards and cubbyholes, now earmarked to start the bonfire. These provoked a shudder: all the memories of terrible Saturday mornings in too-tight collars, knocking on hostile doors in this God-blighted town.

It was the upstairs he was dreading though. He took the bathroom first, the smell of air-freshener lingering – what the hell was the half-life of that stuff – his mam's medicines and make-up stuff quickly into carrier bags. The guest bedroom was quick too, empty and freezing, as he remembered, its wardrobe home to yet more *Watchtowers*.

He faltered in front of his room, 'Deryck's Room' it still said on a china nameplate, except it said 'Derek' not 'Deryck', though he had still been pleased when he'd got it. Fuck, he was tearing up now and he couldn't face what lay inside, the ring-binders, the school-books, the Airfix boats, no, not now, not yet. He went back downstairs, he would clear out those rooms first.

He went into the garden, thinking he'd build a bonfire, except now the rain was coming in from the sea, so instead he just hauled the boxes down the garden, left them in the shed, then walked quickly out of the front door, leaving the place if anything more desolate than it was before. Still, anyone prepared to live on this street, within touching distance of a motorway, would probably be prepared for desolate, thought Deryck, accelerating up to seventy while still on the ramp, his dick hard in his trousers thinking of nothing but speed and power and what he would do to Lianna that night. When he debriefed her. Ha ha.

He could see she was excited soon as he put his head round the door of the North Star, 3 a.m. that night. Looked like a little girl bursting to impress her dad. But he was excited too and he made her wait till after, back at the flat, wait till after his body had stopped shaking from the intensity of it, the fierce bloody abandon, the sheer bloody wrongness of it. Wait till his breathing was normal and his trousers back on before he gave her the opportunity to tell him.

'Look,' she said then, 'you're dead right about this Raj Impex place. Sailor was in last night, right, out of his head, he was, one of these Arab blokes, Yemeni or something, I don't know. Anyway this guy started moaning on to me about how he needed a job and how he'd been dumped here after his last job, been kicked off the boat just 'cause he was bringing in a little blow, "just for my own personal", he said, but like fuck, you know, yeah. Then he says what makes him mad is they're all a bunch of fucking hypocrites, dump him in the shit, call him a drugs smuggler, they're the real smugglers. So I starts listening hard then of course and just casual like ask who the company was and he says fucking Raj Impex, that's who, and I says oh yeah, so what are they smuggling then? And he says people.'

'People,' repeated Deryck, thinking about it.

Made sense. That was where the money was meant to be these days. Well, there was always money in drugs, but people had their advantages: you got paid up front so if they died along the way or got caught the people running the racket still got paid, and if you didn't get them into Britain at the end of the day then that was their tough shit. Not like drugs where that was just stage one. There was no hooking up with heavily armed wholesalers at this end.

'He tell you how it works, the smuggling?'

'No,' said Lianna, 'didn't want to come on like a cop, did I?' She pouted. 'Thought you'd be pleased, I mean you know what to look for now, don't you?'

'Yeah,' said Deryck, 'sorry, yeah, you've done great,' and she looked at him with this puppy-like pleasure that made him feel terrible, at least for a moment, and then ready for round two.

He was just taking the belt from his trousers ready to get started, hardening as he saw the recognition in her eyes, when something dropped from his back pocket and her eyes flicked away from his to see what it was and he turned and looked too and all thoughts of sex began to recede.

It was a copy of the *Watchtower*. He must have picked it up while clearing out his mam's place. He couldn't remember putting it in his pocket but clearly he had. He picked it up again quickly, hoping she wouldn't recognise it for what it was, but too late.

'Bloody hell,' she said, 'you a Jehovah's then?'

'No,' said Deryck, hoping to leave it, but she just kept on looking at him, this smile playing around her lips, and he felt compelled to explain. 'My mother was.'

'Oh,' said Lianna, 'she take you around knocking on doors, did she?'

'Yeah,' said Deryck heavily, 'she did.'

'God, you poor little bastard. So she still into it then, your mum?'

'No,' said Deryck, 'she died last month.'

'Oh,' said Lianna, 'sorry,' and paused for a moment, then her smile returned. 'Still at least she's got her place booked on the giant spaceship to heaven or whatever.'

'Yeah,' said Deryck, 'that's what she thought.' He paused. 'How do you know about it?'

Lianna laughed, picked up the copy of the *Watchtower*. 'Read one of these once, didn't I? So you still a subscriber then?'

'No, I was cleaning out her place yesterday,' he said, then stopped, feeling like he was revealing too much of himself to her, then shook his head at his own foolishness. As if she didn't already know too much about him.

'Poor you,' she said then, and put an arm round him, drew him to her.

He relaxed into the comfort for a moment then pulled

154

away fast, the word mothering flashing across his brain
like a warning, like the open sesame to a world of
locked-down pain.

She looked at him then, startled by the speed of his
withdrawal, but not, he thought, surprised. It was like
she knew him, the real him.

'I'd like to see it,' she said.

He looked at her blankly.

'Your mum's house – the place you come from.'

He didn't respond, just looked at her thinking who are
you – my girlfriend? And then without any conscious
decision he found himself saying, 'OK, that would be
good.'

In work next day the phones were ringing and the paperwork piling up, but he managed to do a little research
lunchtime, checking out the shipping schedules, looking
at the itineraries of the Raj Impex ships, figuring out
possible pick-up points for human cargo, then made some
calls to the Immigration people, see if they'd heard about a
pipeline running through Cardiff, which they said they
hadn't but that didn't mean much, so he said thanks and
wondered whether to take his suspicions to McKenzie
now or wait till he'd got something to back up Lianna's
rumours. He decided to wait – no point in going off half-
cocked and ending up looking like a wanker.

After work he picked up Lianna from her bedsit, just
hit his horn from outside and in seconds she was out and
in the car like she'd been waiting with her coat on for
him.

'Nice car,' she said as she got in, and Deryck grunted and turned up the music and she didn't say anything else till they were on the motorway heading west when she said, 'Christ, we're not going to Swansea are we?' and Deryck had shaken his head, and then when he turned off at Port Talbot she just breathed, 'Oh fucking hell, here.'

'Yeah,' said Deryck, 'here,' and then they were parking the car and walking up the few paces of path, Deryck stooping to pick up a Twix wrapper.

Inside she followed him from front room to kitchen to back room then out through the garden into the shed full of *Watchtowers*.

'What are you going to do with them, burn them?'

Deryck nodded, like yeah, of course, for the first time pleased he'd brought her here. Left to himself he wasn't sure he could have contemplated burning anything.

'This everything? How about upstairs?' she asked him then.

Deryck didn't reply, just led the way back inside and up the stairs, let Lianna open the door to his mam's room, let her suck in her breath as she looked at the cross over the bed, the pictures of Our Lord and Saviour everywhere.

'Fuckin' hell,' she said, 'no wonder your dad fucked off, is it? Not much room for another man in her life.'

Deryck looked at her, immediately suspicious. 'Fuck do you know about my dad?'

Lianna laughed. 'I don't know – where d'you think you're living, boy? It's a small bloody world down the

156

docks – everyone knows who you are, who your dad is. You're not invisible just 'cause you've got a nice flat in the wharf there.'

Deryck thought about that. Contradicted what he'd mostly learned about life, but he realised it was still most likely true. Docks wasn't like normal life. In normal city life you ignore the people around you, they did you the favour of ignoring you right back. Specially if you were a copper. The uniform told them all they needed to know. Even when people got in your face about it, all that sellout shit, they still weren't seeing you the person, they were just seeing a guy in a copper suit. They didn't presume or care to know who you were, where you came from, who your people were. Not till he came back to the docks and then that was all people cared about. Who his dad was, all that shit.

While he stood there immobile, Lianna was going to work, taking down pictures, then the cross. She was about to stick the cross on the pile of junk when she had another idea, turned to him and crudely mimed masturbation, after the fashion of Linda Blair in *The Exorcist*.

'Liked a big one, your mum, eh?'

She smiled at her joke, apparently oblivious to the effect her words were having on Deryck.

'Bet your dad had a big one.'

That did it. Before she knew it Deryck was across the room and slapping her hard across the face and then she gasped with pain and something else and pulled him to her and hissed, 'Big like yours,' in his ear and then he lost it, his control, his self-respect, whatever, and he was doing her right there on his mam's bedroom floor, showing her, letting her feel how big it was, how it could hurt her you put it in the right place, and then finding his mother's dressing-gown cord in his hand – had he picked it up, had Lianna put it there – he didn't know, didn't care, didn't care about anything till the end when he came to and loosed it just in time to let her gasp and gasp for air, her eyes shining, her body still shaking from the ecstatic near-death of it.

And this time he couldn't make himself stand up, dress, compose himself, walk away. This time he needed to be held, cocooned, mothered, no not that please but at least just maybe loved. He needed that and she gave it, she comforted him, let him cry. Crying first for his lost mother, for his hated mother, and for his lost father, hated father, even, and then at last crying for his poor misshapen self, could find love only in anger and violence, crying and thinking he'd never stop till at last she stood up, pulled him up with her and led him out into the garden, where she lit the bonfire with a practised ease that surprised him and loaded the *Watchtowers* on and then the rest of the junk, the clothes and the curtains and the shabby old furniture, the junk that had been a woman's life, his mother's life.

The good stuff she boxed and told him to load up the car and they drove it round to the charity shop and then they came back to the house and he fucked her again, this time without violence or rope or anger but crying all the time, fucking her through a veil of tears, and when they drove back he kept his hand in hers all the way.

★　　★　　★

Back in Cardiff though and the sense of liberation, the joy, quickly faded. Lianna had to go to work, Deryck had an early shift. Be a couple of days before they could get back together.

Deryck did his best to keep his spirits up, went over to the Marina, spent a couple of hours working on the boat, had a quick drink with the feller Pete where all he wanted to do was say I've found her, man, I've found her, the woman can make me whole again, even as he thought it the song coming into his brain and lodging there implacably.

But instead, because this was a feller he only knew from boats, he just talked about GPS systems and water-proof paint and had to get out of there after the one drink and walked home keeping the embers of his exultation going by thinking how one day soon he'd take Lianna out on the boat. And that's what he dreamed of when he slept: a boat and an island and Lianna. He couldn't recapture much of it when he woke, hard as he tried, but those were the essentials.

Then came the early shift and it was difficult to hang on to his patience, much less any exultation. First up were the last of the night's drunks, then the morning's burglary calls and the awful hopeless home visits, finger-printing and asking if people wanted the home-security advisers to come round and bolt the stable door for them, and then did you see the burglar and when they say they did writing down that it was a teenage-to-early-twenties male, short hair, hooded top, dark clothing, white, black or Mediterranean complexion. Worse than useless and all of you knew it and anyway only thing half of them cared about was getting you to give them the case number for the insurance so they could claim for that home cinema set-up they've just remembered they've lost.

Then back to the station for the endless bloody paperwork and then, to cap it all, just as he was in sight of knocking-off time, the call from McKenzie to come into his office.

'How's the investigation going, son?'

'Raj Impex?'

'Yes,' said McKenzie, 'you getting anywhere?'

'Well, sir,' said Deryck carefully, 'I've heard a few rumours but nothing I'd really like to . . .'

'Rumours?' said McKenzie. 'Oh yes?'

'Yes,' said Deryck thinking, Well, he asked for rumours, he can have them. 'I've heard it suggested, sir, that Raj Impex may be involved in people-smuggling.'

'People-smuggling?' echoed McKenzie, making a bit of a show of pondering the idea, folding his hands, staring up at the ceiling. 'Well, they do say that's where the money is these days. And your sources for this information, reliable, are they?'

Deryck shrugged. 'Not sure I could say that, sir, off-duty sailors and so forth, may just be hearsay, may be kosher, who knows at this stage, sir.'

'Who knows, indeed,' said McKenzie, 'but do follow it up. There's a ship coming in next week, I believe, the *Feroza*.'

'Yes, sir,' said Deryck, a little surprised at just how much of an interest McKenzie was clearly taking in the Raj Impex business.

'Well, that would be the time to strike, would it not? D'you need any assistance? I tell you what, I'll put DC Fairfax on the case. He knows the ropes, he'll help you out. Point is I want you to make this a top priority.'

'Yes, sir,' said Deryck once more, and headed back to his desk, wondering more than ever why McKenzie had such a hard-on for Raj Impex.

He checked his watch. Just past four. Had to be a few hours before Lianna started work. He debated whether to go round, ring on her bell, as it were.

Christ, love was weird. Long as he thought all that drew them together, him and Lianna, was lust and anger, mutual loathing turned into sexual energy, it was easy. No problem, no fear, in showing up at the pub, at her house, any time it suited him. Call it love though and he was uncertain, anxious, would he be pushing too hard, all of that confusion that creeps in when you care about the other person instead of simply wanting them.

Love, it was all mess and indecision, everything he hated. And for a long time he'd lived without it. Last time he really felt like this was in school, Denise Bradley. Puppy love, let me carry your books home love, school dance love, Aberavon Beach at night love, sitting on the benches outside the café love, in the park after dark with a broken condom love, getting a hiding off Denise's dad love, get the fuck away from my daughter you bastard love.

Since then, though, he'd wised up, hardened up, learnt that dislike, even contempt, won fair lady as often as not. Learnt that contempt and anger made it better for both of you, learnt that he liked to hurt and some of them liked to be hurt, and then if you couldn't find one that did, you could always pay one.

And he knew it was wrong. Or maybe not wrong exactly – who knew what right and wrong were? He certainly didn't and he was a copper. In fact the longer he was a copper the less he knew. What he knew instead was the law. But if not wrong, he knew at least it was not . . . not helping him. It was . . . it was decaying him, he thought. Like *9½ Weeks*, you know, the Mickey Rourke guy, that's how he felt sometimes. All cool and buttoned-up and in control but doomed to repeat the same scenarios over and over. For the girl it was an adventure, a journey to some dark continent, for the bloke, the sadist, if you like – and of course it didn't have to be the bloke, he supposed – it was a life sentence.

And now this unexpected freedom was leaving him paralysed, caught in the headlights, unable to direct his footsteps east or west. In the end he let them take him west, over the bridge into Grangetown. Only she wasn't in. Which was fair enough. Why should she be? She could be shopping or doing her laundry or round her friend's place or simply taking a walk to get away from her depressing bedsit.

Before, he wouldn't have given it a moment's thought. Now, with his lover's shoes having brought him to her door, he was paranoid. Did she have another boyfriend – one who hadn't wooed her by beating and choking her? Worse: had she gone for good, freaked out at their intimacy? Was she a commitment phobe, if that was what they call them on *Oprah*? How could he know?

He waited for a few minutes, bought an *Echo* from the newsagent, tried to tell himself he needed to get a few things from the chemist, rang the bell again. Why didn't she have a mobile? Surely in the age of the mobile there was no need for this kind of foolishness. He could give her one, or would that be excessive? Maybe she already had one, just hadn't given him the number. Had he ever asked her? He didn't think so.

Finally, he let his lover's shoes beat the retreat over the bridge. He picked up his car from the station, narrowly avoiding bumping into Jimmy Fairfax and McKenzie in the process, thought about going down to the Marina for a bit, but right then the heavens opened and he headed home instead, and was just midway through chopping up some carrots to put in his juicer when the intercom buzzed.

'Hi,' said a voice, Lianna. 'I was just on my way to work. Is it OK if . . .'

'Yes,' said Deryck 'of course, get the lift to the second floor,' and buzzed her in, and moments later here she was inside his nice, pristine flat.

'Gorgeous,' she said, setting her bag down in the middle of the living area and looking around, 'gorgeous.'

'Yeah,' said Deryck, 'I like it.' He just stood there for a moment looking at her standing there, the line of her body tall and elegant, the clothes she had on something less than elegant. He talked to dispel the gathering awkwardness. 'You like a drink or something?'

'No thanks,' she said, 'really I've got to be in work in a sec. I was just wondering, you know, how you were.'

Now the awkwardness was well and truly there. Before, any time they'd been together this long in private, Deryck had been all over her, ordering her, making her, doing her. Now he didn't know what he was meant to do. Kiss her? Tell her about his day?

Out of nowhere some more words came out. 'You want to go sailing with me tomorrow?'

Her eyes widened. 'You got a boat?'

'Yeah,' said Deryck, 'I've got a boat.'

'Love to,' she said, and picked up her bag, darted towards him and kissed him on the lips.

He grabbed hold of her then, pulled her to him roughly, bit down on her lip to the point of pain. She pulled away then, her breathing starting to turn ragged.

'Tomorrow,' she said. 'What time?'

Deryck thought about it. He was doing a night shift tomorrow, which was perfect. 'Eleven,' he said, 'I'll pick you up,' and she smiled and waved and when she was gone he drank down his carrot juice without even wincing once.

After an evening spent plotting possible sailing plans and a night spent dreaming of drowning and saving – him or her, he couldn't say; there seemed to be a constant elision between them in his dreams, as if he no longer knew whether he was subject or object – Deryck had got up early, worked out a little on his fitness bench, juiced some oranges, eaten a decent breakfast and headed over to the Marina, to make sure everything was just so.

Eleven on the dot he was ringing her bell, bringing her bleary-eyed to the door. Five minutes then, waiting for her to get herself together, and they drove round to the Marina.

He was nervous showing her the boat. You never knew what people expected, you told them you had a boat. Mostly they either imagined a luxury yacht or a rubber dinghy, not something like this – a twelve-foot sailing dinghy. Lianna though seemed to be the exception to the rule, just said nice boat and looked inside, asked if he ever slept on it and Deryck said only when I've had to and they both laughed as if he'd made a joke which he hadn't really and then he started getting ready for the off and Lianna amazingly didn't get in the way, didn't ask stupid questions, and helped when he asked her to. By the time they had the boat on the water he was practically ready to marry her. Christ, he thought, he had really better start getting a grip.

For this first trip he had originally been thinking about heading out past the barrage, swinging around to Penarth, or even over to Flatholm, the little island four miles into the Channel, but the wind was up gale force three to four with a possibility of five later on so instead they were just going to take a turn round the inner harbour then back up the River Ely.

'Wow,' said Lianna as they got close to the barrage, 'I hadn't realised how big it was.'

Deryck nodded. It was true, from a distance the

barrage didn't look like much, just another dock wall; up close and you could see it had been an enormous undertaking. A billion pounds he'd read they spent on turning the docks into a lake, and most of it had gone on this one mighty structure.

Before they got too close though, he swung the boat round to starboard, heading towards the Penarth Marina, the beginning of the Ely. He adjusted the sail as the wind actually seemed to be dying down, nothing more than a two now, just a breeze really, and soon he had time to turn his attention to his passenger.

'Enjoying it?' he asked.

'Yeah,' she said, smiling back at him, ' 's'great. You go out to sea in this?'

'Yeah,' said Deryck, 'well, you know, along the coast.'

'Oh yeah,' said Lianna sounding interested, 'where-abouts?'

'Oh,' said Deryck doing his best to sound casual, 'round the Gower, Milford, across the Channel, Devon coast, Cornwall, you know.'

'Great,' said Lianna, 'I'd love to go with you some time,' standing up now, her head thrown back, feeling the breeze on her face.

'Great,' said Deryck too, then, 'I'd like that,' his enthusiasm just a little tempered by a small dissenting voice in the back of his head wondering if all this wasn't a bit too good to be true.

No one could be this right for him. Remember who she was: she might like rough sex and sailing, she might seem to see through to his hidden depths, she was still a lowlife barmaid, one step up from a hooker. Not the kind of girl he could ever have taken back to . . . no, don't think about that. What did he want to do? Fuck up a perfectly good thing? And, anyway, here on the boat she didn't seem like the bar girl he'd taken her for. Even her voice sounded different. Her voice which was now talking to him.

'I heard some more about Raj Impex last night,' she was saying.

His brain snapped to attention. 'Oh yes?'

'Yeah, one of the sailor boys was in last night. Waris his name is, and he was completely wasted, trying to get all the girls to go with him, except he didn't have any money so he comes over to me at the bar, starts slobbering all over me, you know, thinking he can't afford to pay for it, maybe I'll give him a freebie. In his dreams, yeah, but anyway he gets talking about how he's missing being at sea and how he's got a girlfriend in Larnaca and how he's pissed off 'cause he should be out there now except they didn't want him to go this time – "Wanted my passport, not me," he said, and I said, "Oh yeah?" and he says, "Yeah, feller will be using it on the way back," and he's not making a lot of sense but I think I figured out what he meant – they go out with like say twelve crew listed but really there's only ten crew and two spare passports from sailors who've stayed home, they pick up a couple of extra guys somewhere on the way and all of a sudden there's twelve crew after all. Or twenty or thirty or whatever. You see what I'm saying?'

Deryck thought about it, thought about it and liked it.

'Christ, girl,' he said, 'you're the one should be a copper, you're a bloody genius, you are.'

The rest of the way back to the Marina he thought about it. What a nice simple scam. Elegant even. The crew of the *Feroza* wouldn't be smuggling contraband, they would be the contraband. Hard to see it wouldn't work, specially somewhere like Cardiff, frankly a bit of a backwater these days.

Only thing that nagged him was surely you couldn't bring in too many people at a time that way. Three or four, maybe half a dozen tops, given that there had to be certain amount of crew could actually man the ship. So they'd have to be paying a fair few quid to make it worthwhile. So, so, maybe these were the kind of people could afford to spend a bit, though that didn't really make sense either seeing as, far as Deryck understood, the Immigration policy was if you were rich you were welcome here, it was only the poor we were busy keeping out.

Unless . . . unless there were other reasons these people didn't want to go through Immigration. Deryck took a sharp intake of breath. He read the papers, he watched the news. Imagine it. A fucking al-Qa'ida pipeline into Cardiff and he, Deryck Douglas, the man who stopped it. He allowed the fantasy to take shape for a moment then shook his head – getting way ahead of himself here.

And then they were back at the Marina. Deryck jumped to shore as they got close and tied up. As he fastened the rope he caught Lianna's eyes on him. As he pulled the knot tight she smiled, licked her lips, and suddenly he had the old hunger back.

As he helped Lianna out of the boat she leaned into him, whispered your place in his ear, and he nodded and in no time they were back there and he was having her, doing her, on his nice shiny hardwood floor and afterwards he didn't cry or break down and she turned to him and said, 'Thank fuck for that, thought you'd gone soft on me,' and she smiled at him, teeth bared, eyes shining, all hard selfish desire, just briefly sated, and said, 'You got anything to drink?' and he went to the fridge and brought out a bottle of New Zealand white and put 'Live in Paris' on the CD player and she laughed and said, 'Mr Smooth,' and he laughed and then she said, 'So you going to nail the bastard then?' and Deryck, surprised for a second, said, 'Nail what bastard?' and she said, 'Val Dennison, that bastard, the Raj Impex one,' and he braced himself, ready for who knew what revelation, and said, 'So you going to tell me what this is about, you and Val Dennison?'

'OK,' she said slowly, 'he killed my sister.'

Deryck just sat there staring at her. What the fuck? 'You what?' he said finally.

'What I said – Val Dennison murdered my sister. And the bastard coppers – no reflection on you – didn't do a bloody thing about it.'

'Whoah,' said Deryck then, 'just go slow, yeah? And fill me in a bit – for starters, who's your sister?'

'My sister,' said Lianna quietly, 'her name is, was, Julie, she was married to the bastard Val. You must have heard what happened, how the bastard drowned her. And no one did anything, just took his word for it. Well, maybe I'm going to do something.'

Deryck didn't say anything, just stood up walked over to the window trying to make sense of this, make sense of her.

'So,' he said finally, 'is that why you're working in that place?'

'Yeah,' said Lianna, 'well, I needed a job anyway, and I thought maybe I'd find something out. I don't know what I thought really.'

Deryck stared at her. Part of him felt pleased, happy to find his girl wasn't just a lowlife barmaid. The copper part of him, though, was watchful, didn't like people turning out to be something different from what they presented themselves as.

'And what about me then? Am I just part of your plan?'

She looked startled by this. 'God no,' she said, 'you, well, you know how you got to me' – she rubbed her neck slowly – 'don't you? And I couldn't believe it when you told me you're investigating Raj Impex. It's just like – what's the word? – synchronicity.'

Synchronicity. Wasn't something the copper in Deryck had much time for, but for once the lover was in charge and the lover would settle for synchronicity. For now at least.

In work that night the first person Deryck ran into was Jimmy Fairfax.

'Del,' said Jimmy. 'Wassup? How's my new partner doing?'

Deryck looked at him blankly for a moment then remembered. McKenzie had said he'd ask Jimmy to help out with the Raj Impex business.

'Yeah, all right,' he said. 'Boss filled you in then, has he?'

Jimmy shrugged. 'Yeah, sort of. Said you reckoned they were into people-smuggling. That right?'

Deryck's turn to shrug. 'Maybe; it's a rumour I've heard.'

'Oh yeah,' said Jimmy, 'who from?'

'One of my informants,' said Deryck, hoping Jimmy would leave it there.

'Oh aye,' said Jimmy, 'this the kind of informant got the nice tits and works in the North Star?'

Deryck didn't say anything, which pretty much gave the game away.

'So where did she hear this rumour? One of the sailors?'

'Yeah,' said Deryck, 'that's right.'

'What d'you reckon?'

Deryck pursed his lips. 'Hard to say. Seems possible.'

'S'pose,' said Jimmy. And then, of course, 'Meant to be where the money is these days. When's the ship getting in?'

'Wednesday.'

'Better get a move on then. Any idea how they're working it? Stuck the poor buggers in containers or what?'

Deryck paused then decided not to share the crew-swap theory just yet. One thing he'd learned, you wanted to get on in this job you didn't go sharing too much in the way of vital information till the last moment. 'Dunno,' he said, 'maybe.'

'Well,' said Jimmy, 'let's get out there, rattle a few cages.'

Deryck sighed inwardly, suspecting he knew what that meant – a subsidised pub crawl – but couldn't think up a decent excuse to opt out. And indeed the next couple of hours saw them hit the Packet, the White Hart, the Ship and Pilot and the Sea Lock. Jimmy had a whisky in each and Deryck a Coke and Jimmy glad-handed and bull-shitted and got, as far as Deryck could see, precisely nowhere.

No one seemed to have heard anything about Raj Impex or the *Feroza* except for the ones who – because you'd asked them the question – would immediately figure out what you were angling towards, and so they'd say something pensive like, 'Smuggling, yeah?' and you'd say, 'Yeah, what d'you know about it?' and they'd say, 'No, boss, thought you knew something about it. What's it they smuggling then? Charlie? Fags?' All a pointless, irritating waste of time and Deryck was thrilled when closing time fell in the Sea Lock.

'Right then, back to the station, yeah,' he said to Jimmy, but Jimmy just grins and says, 'Not yet, Del boy, the night is young,' and for an awful moment Deryck thought he was going to demand they went to the North Star, but instead he says, 'Soca night at the Big Windsor.

The old-timers will be out raving it up. Let's see what's what.'

The Big Windsor was an imposing old wreck of a pub down by the dockside. Apparently back in the day it had been a flash place with a smart restaurant, place all the docks moneymen went. These days though it looked semi-derelict. There was no sign on the door and, as they walked in, you could sense this was a place on its last legs, just waiting for the brewery to pull the plug, close it down till such time as the docklands revival made it worth refurbishing.

Deryck looked around at the place while Jimmy had a word with the middle-aged feller on the door. Place was about half-full. Mostly, like Jimmy had said, an older crowd. Old-time docks people, the kind Deryck half remembered from being a kid. Black and white but mostly kind of a light-brown. Except they all seemed like they fitted in here and Deryck had never for a moment felt like he fitted in anywhere.

His conversation finished, Jimmy rejoined him. 'Christ,' he said, 'you are one seriously cold bastard, you know that, Del?'

Deryck looked at Jimmy blankly.

'Ignoring your own father like that.'

Deryck stared at Jimmy, looking for any sign that this might be a put-on, but couldn't find one.

'Jesus,' said Jimmy, 'your face. Christ, man, didn't you recognise him? Shit, I'm sorry . . .'

But Deryck wasn't listening to Jimmy's blather, he was

manoeuvring himself so he could stare unnoticed at the man on the door, the father he hadn't seen in what, eighteen years.

And what he saw wasn't the ogre his mother had portrayed, the impossibly handsome, impossibly uncaring brute of her stories. Neither was he the great looming presence Deryck remembered from his childhood. For starters he was smaller than Deryck now. He was just another bloke, fifty or so, a cheery-looking feller still hanging on, Deryck could see, to some kind of dandyism, still wearing a suit and a porkpie hat but really just another feller in the bookie's with a laugh and a twinkle for the ladies and a bottle of Dragon Stout never too far from the hand.

Deryck turned back to Jimmy. 'Does he know who I am?'

Jimmy laughed, 'Course he does, Del, everyone knows who you are. You're a Docks boy, you like it or not. Now go say hello to your old man. I'll be at the bar.' And with that Jimmy gave Deryck a shove in the back, sent him straight into his dad, Cyril's line of sight, and Deryck had no choice but to keep on going, meet his father's gaze.

Up close there was no doubting it. It was less a matter of visual recognition than whole-body recognition. He could feel himself shaking, willed himself to stay calm.

'Hello,' he said sticking out a hand to forestall any possibility that his old man might try to hug him, but Cyril just nodded, smiled an infuriating I understand the world better than you ever will smile, and lazily stuck his hand out.

'Heard you was back in town, boy,' he said.

'Yeah,' said Deryck, standing there feeling stupid as another gaggle of punters came in through the door started gabbing to his father while he stood there like a spare part, only to feel even more uncomfortable when Cyril turned and told the incomers, church ladies done up in their Saturday-night finery, 'An' here's me boy Deryck, y'know, the policeman,' and the ladies fell on him with a welter of, 'I remember you when you were just a little pickney boy,' and, 'How's you mother, darlin', she doing all right?' and Deryck just standing there nodding like an idiot, not saying his mother was dead, not really saying anything, just wanting them to go, which at last they did, leaving him once more standing with his father.

'So, son, you liking it in the force?' Again the grin that made Deryck feel like whatever he said, he would be making himself ridiculous.

'S'OK,' he said. 'How about you?' He paused, catching himself about to say Dad, and aborting the word at the last minute. 'You working these days?'

'Bits and pieces, boy, you know how it is. Hear they've got you running round looking at ships.'

'Hmm,' said Deryck, wondering what he was getting at.

'You looking for smugglers, boy, that what it is?'

Deryck shrugged, not really taking in the question at first, just resolving that if this so-called father of his called him boy one more time he would slap him upside the head, then registering the sense of what he'd said and thinking, What the hell?

Then, before he could follow it up, a next wave of new arrivals came through the door and his dad turned his attention to them, casual as you like, and Deryck walked over towards the bar, thinking, Is that it? All those years he'd wondered what it would be like if he saw his father again and the guy just acted like Deryck had never been away, popped out for a bag of sweets and just took a bit of time over it.

Maybe that's what it was, maybe time had stood still in this backwater. Far as Cyril knew Bob Marley was still alive and so was Deryck's mum. Bastard hadn't even mentioned her, no how's Iris, how's your mum, nothing. A wave of anger came over him, made him stop in his tracks before he got to the bar, remembrance of when he was fourteen and he used to fantasise about killing his father – this is for Mum and this and this and this is for turning her into a religious nutter, and this is for leaving me with her.

He took a deep breath, moved on, saw Jimmy in the midst of a bunch of ageing lads with prison tats and bench-press muscles. He was sure he saw Jimmy slip something into his pocket as he approached. What a fucking circus. Jimmy Fairfax, Cyril bloody Douglas, all of them happily living in the moment, not giving a shit about anything or anyone but themselves.

'I'm off,' he said to Jimmy. 'See you back at the station,' and walked off without even a glance at any of Jimmy's mates.

He knew Jimmy would be staring after him with a what's the matter with you, pal? expression on his face but right now Deryck just needed to be out of this place, out of earshot of the maddening bloody soca beat, away from the stink of booze and fags and ganja, the air his dad breathed. He felt like it was choking him: walked straight out of the Big Windsor and gulped in great lungfuls of sea air.

He started walking back to the station, but couldn't face the thought of more people, more nicotine-flavoured air, sweat and fear on one floor, stewed tea and rancid pastries on the other, and instead decided to head over to the docks proper, have a little look at Raj Impex. What he expected to find there in the middle of the night he didn't know, didn't really care, the walk was the thing.

In fact, so bound up was he in trying to make some sense, any sense, of his utterly anti-climactic meeting with his father that he almost walked past the Raj Impex building. It was only the light coming from the back office that attracted his attention, all the other warehouse buildings being completely dark, the only illumination coming from the moon and the searchlights trained on a boat over in Queen Alexandra Dock.

Deryck moved carefully towards the Raj Impex building. He couldn't get close to the lit window; the car park was in the way and its chain-link fence locked. Inside the car park, though, he could see Spiller's Merc, which suggested at least that the light wasn't down to burglars, just the boss man doing some overtime. Which was fair enough: maybe that's how he got his Merc, burning the midnight oil, going the extra mile for his customers, all that good stuff. He walked round the car park, trying to find an angle that would let him see clearly into the office. No luck, but just as he was retracing his steps the office light went out and Deryck withdrew to the shadows.

Moments later the back door opened and out came a man, and another figure, looked to be a woman. As the man locked the door a security light came on, back-lighting the two figures. The bloke's face was still shadowed but, seeing as he was unlocking Spiller's car, Deryck reasonably enough decided he must be Spiller. Then the woman came round the back of the car and it was only as she ducked to get into the passenger door that Deryck got a glimpse of her face. It was enough though to make his heart jump. What the hell was Lianna doing getting into Spiller's car?

It was a question that was driven to the back of his mind for a while though, as the minute Deryck walked back into the station he found the place in a frenzy of activity. There'd been a shooting on Dumballs Road outside a car re-sprayer's. And it was only Craig Ibadulla, wasn't it, who'd taken the bullet high up his right arm.

Craig was one of Kenny Ibadulla's cousins, an up-and-comer on the gangster scene, and of course he wasn't saying a word, but lo and behold there was even a witness – some yuppie driving back to his gated community further down Dumballs had seen the garage door open, two men walk out – Craig and another feller – and then he'd seen some guy lean out of the window of a parked car and shoot at Craig before speeding off.

The car was a silver Audi TT, yuppie had no trouble recognising one of them, and he even had a partial on the number plate. So every patrol car for miles around was busy keeping their eyes open and all Craig's known associates were being given a 4 a.m. wake-up call.

Deryck got stuck with checking out who owned the garage, which was next to impossible in the middle of the night, then going down the hospital to try and get something out of Craig while he was still in shock. Except Craig was one of those guys who wouldn't be in shock if you put a pound of Semtex in his toilet, so that was a bit of a bust too, but still one way or another Deryck didn't have a minute to think about Lianna till he made it back to his flat around seven feeling utterly knackered and equally sure that he had no chance of sleeping.

A couple of hours of fruitlessly trying and he gave up the unequal struggle, got dressed again and went round to Lianna's place determined to have this out right away. One useful thing he'd learned as a copper was there was no point wasting your time speculating about things when you could just go and ask people.

Took a while for Lianna to answer his ringing and when she did at last come down to the door, wrapped in a sky-blue bathrobe, she looked about as tired as he felt. One look at Deryck standing there on her doorstep with a face like thunder though, and the bleariness left her eyes, her tongue flickered between her lips and she pulled him inside, her bathrobe falling open as she did so, apparently completely oblivious to who might be looking.

Deryck tried to resist her. Pulled his mouth away from hers, but followed her indoors anyway to avoid scandalising the street. As the street door closed though she pulled the cord from her bathrobe and offered it to him and all thoughts of resistance became inaudible, scrambled by the white noise of lust.

Afterwards though, before he'd even untied her hands, he got straight to it. 'What were you doing at Raj Impex last night?'

She flinched at that, which was something. Didn't flinch if you slapped her, this Lianna, but catching her off-guard, that had done it. She mumbled something, sounded like, 'Blah blah told me.'

'What?' he said roughly, feeling the return of the fierce selfish nihilistic joy he'd felt when he'd first been with her, feeling all that life-affirming lovey-dovey crap slip away.

'You told me to,' she said.

'Sorry?'

'You told me to,' she repeated, 'told me to find out about Raj Impex.'

He looked at her, disbelieving. 'Oh yeah, so you just popped round there, middle of the night, and there was John Spiller waiting to have a nice chat with some slag he doesn't know from Adam.'

He saw her flinch again at his words, could see he was hurting her. Well, fuck her, she was a lying whore, they all were.

'But he does know me. I met him a few times at Val's place.'

Deryck stared at her, more confused than angry now. Somehow he'd forgotten her Dennison connection. He was tired, his head hurt, his body was crying out for postcoital rest, but he still had to find out what was going on here.

'You mind untying me?' said Lianna then.

Deryck shook his head hard, trying to wake up some brain cells, then undid the rope. He waited for her to rub the soreness out of her wrists then asked the one question his exhausted brain was capable of phrasing. 'You mind telling me what the fuck is going on?'

'OK,' said Lianna, adjusting herself so she was sitting up on the bed, her back resting against the wall. 'It's like I told you. Julie Dennison was my sister. He treated her like, like you wouldn't treat a dog, beat her, cheated on her, you name it. Why'd she stay with him? Well, he was rich, for one thing, and he was a bastard for another thing. You may not have noticed but some women like bastards. Doesn't feel real, they're not getting hit.'

She paused, her eyes boring into Deryck's guilty soul. 'Anyway, then she drowned and I know it was down to him. I just know it, right, don't ask how. I knew her and I know him and that's what happened, don't care what the inquest said. I know, right? So I came down here, right? We're not from here, me and Jule. Gloucester is where we're from and I got this job and I'm waiting for him, I'm ready for him, and when he gets off that boat – that's why I went to see Spiller, find out when the boat's coming in – when that boat comes in, you know what I'm going to do? I'm going to kill him.'

'Fuck's sake,' said Deryck, his stare now accompanied by an open mouth, and then a pure copper's question, not why or are you nuts but, 'How?'

And just like that she stuck her hand under the mattress and brought out a gun; looked to Deryck, who was no expert, like a Beretta.

'Jesus Christ,' he said, looking her in the eyes and seeing absolutely nothing to suggest she was either joking or incapable of carrying through on her words, 'Jesus Christ.'

'Three days' time,' she said, 'three days' time when Val Dennison gets off that boat I'm going to kill him.'

Deryck thought about going for the gun, wrestling it away from her, decided against it, opted for an attempt at rational argument instead. 'And then what? You want to go to prison?'

'No,' said Lianna, 'I want to die too.' She held the gun close to her chest.

As she said those words though, Deryck flashed, not on Lianna on the dockside shooting down Val Dennison then herself, but on his mother in hospital uttering those same words, 'I want to die,' and with the same kind of desperate joy, fuelled in her case by the fantasy of going to Jehovah. With Lianna it was something else but whatever it was right now it was too much for Deryck to take. Without another word he pulled on the rest of his clothes and left.

Back in his flat, stretched out on the bed vainly trying at least to get some rest before going into work, Deryck tried to make some sense of the situation. He didn't doubt for a minute that Lianna would try to kill Dennison and part of him felt almost cheered by the revelation that this was her plan. Like she may be a crazy, would-be killer but at least she's not two-timing me.

Question was how to stop her. The answer was simple really – raid the boat when it came in, round up the illegals, and bust the ringleaders – Spiller on shore and Val Dennison off the boat. Leaving no chance for Lianna to shoot him and hopefully once she saw him locked up that would satisfy her.

Simple really: all he had to do was persuade McKenzie to launch the raid. And even that shouldn't be too hard. After all it was McKenzie's baby, the whole Raj Impex business, right from the start. All Deryck needed to do was tell him how they were working it, swapping crew for illegals. He'd been hoping to get a bit more corroboration before he presented it to the boss, but needs must.

Deryck got up, made himself a pot of coffee, put on Cassandra Wilson for a change, and by the time he got to work he was feeling thoroughly energised, for all his lack of sleep.

And sure enough, soon as Deryck laid out the Raj Impex scam, McKenzie was right up for it. Got it straight away, then congratulated Deryck, went into a lot of blather about what a great asset to the team he was – 'Useless bastards have been looking into Raj for years, haven't found a thing, you come here and in two weeks you've laid the whole thing open' – and Deryck smiled and looked modest but couldn't resist punching the air when he got back to his desk armed with the news that he was to be in charge of the team who would meet the *Feroza* as it came in from sea, bust the Raj Impex scam wide open.

Wednesday morning, the day of the raid, Deryck woke early, just after six. He got up carefully, making sure not to wake Lianna, who was snoring gently in the bed next to him. The ship wasn't due in till four that afternoon and he wasn't due in work till ten, but before he started he wanted to think things through carefully, by himself.

On the face of it, it was simple. Be there waiting for the boat, wait till they get the gang plank sorted out, swarm on board, take names, check passports, find out just who wasn't who. Make sure there's a couple of officers waiting on shore case anyone tries to sneak off, couple more waiting in case anyone's crazy enough to try jumping off the side. It was simple.

But Deryck had been a policeman for long enough to know that there's no such thing as simple, something his first guv'nor, feller called Hardy back in Swansea, used to say. Ships were big places, plenty of places to hide, and then you've got a bunch of blokes who come from four corners of the earth, most of them no doubt pretending they can't speak English the moment there's any trouble. Need a cool head keeping control of the situation.

And then, even if they do find the ringers, chances are they'll claim political asylum right away, so the Immigration fellers will have to come on board, sort all that

out. He'd alerted Special Branch who were dead interested – he could hear them down the phone thinking al-
Qa'ida to themselves. So even if the whole thing worked
out perfectly it would still be a job keeping any of the
credit for it himself. However much the brass muscled in
on it, though, he was sure it had to be enough to get him
what he wanted. A transfer out of Butetown for good.
Get Lianna out as well.

Lianna. What was going on with her he just didn't
know. The last couple of days after her big outburst,
she'd calmed right down, said she was sorry, said she
was upset, said she didn't mean it, obviously knew
she'd gone too far. But did he believe her? Did he
believe, if she could see Val Dennison out of the
window right now, she would leave him be? He
was nowhere near sure of that. He was nowhere near
sure of anything with Lianna. Not true, there were
moments with her he was sure he felt better, felt
stronger, felt like he could reconcile himself with
the universe – if that didn't sound too dumb to think,
let alone speak. What it was, some moments with her,
he felt comfortable in his skin. Trouble was those
moments were always during sex. And how far could
you ever trust sex?

He looked back at her, sleeping on his bed. He hadn't
seen her for two days, their shifts out of sync, and then
she turned up the night before, 3.30 a.m. straight from
work, knowing it was the night before the ship came in,
of course, she must have known that, and he'd let her in
still half-asleep and she'd been fierce with her need and it

had taken him a minute or two to get into it, still full of the softness of sleep, and her fierceness had turned ferocious and he'd been scared for a moment – the masochist scaring the sadist, the desire to be hurt stronger than the desire to hurt. Probably that said something about life in general, Deryck thought now in the calm light of morning, but then it had scared him then angered him and so lit the blue touch paper and they'd been away and afterwards she'd slept like a baby and he dreamed and woke, dreamed and woke.

And now he was ready and he would nail Val Dennison before Lianna could get anywhere near him and then she'd see that Deryck was the one in control and then maybe they could find out whether what they had in bed had a future outside it.

He was making a third cup of coffee when the intercom went. The noise of it woke Lianna – he could hear a stirring from the bedroom as he walked over to the intercom, said hello.

'That Deryck?' said a voice, a seldom-heard, too familiar voice, the voice of Cyril, Deryck amazed to find he knew it at once.

'Yeah,' said Deryck, 'what do you want?'

'Let me in, boy, got something you need to hear.'

Deryck closed his eyes. If there was anything he needed less than this he couldn't imagine it. He sighed and said, 'Second floor,' and pressed the buzzer to open the door.

As he did so Lianna popped her head out of the bedroom. 'What's up?' she asked.

'Nothing,' said Deryck, 'just someone coming round for a minute. You mind staying there?'

'What,' said Lianna, 'don't want your friends to see me naked?' Then she smiled and closed the door.

And Deryck found himself staring at the closed door for a few seconds, his mind blanking out rather than contemplate the imminent arrival of his dad. He willed himself back into life then went out into the hall, saw his dad walking up the stairs, ushered him in.

'You want coffee?'

'Yeah,' said his dad, 'be nice,' and Deryck poured him a cup and watched his dad roaming around the room looking at things and nodding to himself and then he handed over the cup and they sat down, his dad on the sofa, Deryck on an office chair, and his dad sipped the coffee, then said, 'You're looking into this Raj Impex business, yeah?'

Deryck nodded, wondering what the hell was coming next – don't tell him, oh god don't tell him his dad was involved in the scam and had come round to ask him to drop the investigation. Christ, that would be something. Just the thought of it stirred up wildly conflicting emotions. Half of Deryck was just dying to see the look on his dad's face when he told him the raid couldn't be stopped, half of him just felt sorry for the old man coming by on such a pitiful errand.

Except that wasn't what Cyril had come to say. What Cyril had come to say was, 'Be careful.'

'Sorry,' said Deryck, 'careful of what?' Then he

thought he got it. 'You threatening me or something? Your gangster friends send you round to warn me off?'

'Jesus boy, did you mama raise you for a fool? I'm not threatening you, boy, and I'm not no raasclaat gangster. I'm warning you 'cause you're my boy. I'm telling you to be careful 'cause what everyone says is Raj Impex is police-protected.'

Deryck exhaled slowly. Trying this notion out. Could it be true? Well, course it could be true, in the abstract at least. Deryck wasn't naive, he heard the rumours, he'd seen the coppers take early retirement on the Costa del Crime. But this time he couldn't see it. They were raiding the ship, any protection Raj Impex might have had had obviously run out, end of story. That said, if there were any officers looking to fuck the raid up, well, that was worth knowing about in advance, one more thing to put into his bumper bag of worries for the afternoon's raids.

'Yeah?' he said finally. 'You got any names?'

His dad looked at him, lips pursed, and then, before he could say anything else, the bedroom door opened.

Deryck whirled round to see Lianna ostentatiously tiptoeing towards the kitchen area. At least she was dressed. But whatever Cyril might have been about to say, the sight of Lianna put a stop to it.

Instead he stood up, said, 'Didn't know you were keeping company, son,' and without another word to Deryck, or any word at all to Lianna, he walked out.

Lianna waited till the door had shut behind him, then turned to Deryck. 'Who was that then?'

Deryck just shook his head. 'Nobody,' he said, 'just an informant.'

The ship was late. It had been due in twenty minutes ago. There'd been radio contact with the port office confirming their course and arrival time an hour or so before and they were already into the Bristol Channel. Deryck was starting to get antsy. Everything was in place. They'd waited till the last minute before busting into Raj Impex, where they'd arrested John Spiller, who was raising all hell, but once you got the Immigration people working with you the powers you had were extraordinary. Made the laws up as they went along, those fellers.

Dockside everything looked nice and normal, fellers were there ready to fix up the gang plank and whatever, start unloading, and waiting in the warehouse were the team – half a dozen regular coppers under Deryck's command, Immigration officers, and two Special Branch guys, one of whom was an old mate of Jimmy's, which for once was a bit of a blessing 'cause it stopped them from coming over all superior. Now all they needed was the bastard boat to show up.

Nightmare scenarios started to run through Deryck's brain. The ship had been spooked by something – maybe some special code they were expecting from Spiller hadn't been given and they'd headed for Avonmouth or Newport or somewhere and were busy unloading the cargo while Deryck sat here on the dockside looking like an idiot. Or maybe they'd had an accident, the ship was sinking out there in the Channel. Something like that happened there'd be such chaos they'd probably never sort out who was who.

And what about Lianna? For a moment he turned his gaze from the Channel – which he was scanning for any sign of the *Feroza* – to the port behind him. As if he'd spot Lianna hiding in the bushes with a sniper rifle. Christ, he hated waiting.

His phone went off in his jacket pocket. Probably McKenzie wanting to know what the fuck was going on. But it wasn't, it was the harbourmaster. The *Feroza* was just coming alongside the Barrage now: five minutes to docking. Deryck switched his gaze back round to the Channel. He could see it now, a boat just emerging from the shadow of the Penarth outcrop. He went back into the warehouse, found Jimmy leading the coppers and the Branch guys in a game of cards, the Immigration weirdos just standing there like lemons.

'C'mon lads,' he said. 'Five minutes.'

Five minutes of pure anticipation and excitement. Five minutes of imagining the kudos he'd receive for pulling this off. Five minutes of living in fantasy land. Five minutes before it all started going to hell.

He could smell it in the minute the boat docked and they all swarmed on. No one seemed alarmed or scared or, worst of all, even surprised.

He'd been expecting chaos, the ship in panic as soon as they saw the police getting on board. Then it struck him maybe they were expecting another drugs bust, thought the cops were here to check through a bunch of containers full of the ugliest furniture known to mankind. Well, maybe they'd feel a bit different when they found out what he was really after.

There was a Middle Eastern feller who came up to meet Deryck and his landing party on the foredeck, looked like he was in charge. Must be the captain, Deryck figured.

'You Mr Omar?'

'Yeah,' said the feller, his accent local. Not Cardiff, Newport maybe. 'What can I do for you, boss?'

'Looking for Val Dennison,' said Deryck, figuring it was the organ grinder he needed to talk to, not the monkey.

Omar shook his head. 'Val got off at Porto, should be back here by now.'

'You what?'

'Yeah, had some business to do.'

Deryck frowned, wondering what that meant, something or nothing. Well, at least it meant he wasn't around to get shot by Lianna. He just hoped no one else got off at Porto.

'Need to see the crew register,' he said then. 'Get them all assembled here, please, for an Immigration check.'

Deryck watched the feller's eyes as he said this, looking for a sign, a flicker of panic. Didn't get one.

The bastard just nodded, said, 'Sure, five minutes, boss,' and once again Deryck had the sinking feeling.

It took ten minutes in the end but finally they were all assembled. Fifteen men, mostly Middle Eastern, a couple of Poles, a probable Tamil and the rest local boys.

First thing Deryck noticed when he looked at the crew list was that there was no sign of the name Lianna had given him – Waris, she told him the guy in the North Star was called – and the name Waris Hussein was on the list Deryck had seen filed with the port authority. Wasn't on this list though.

'Where's Waris Hussein?' said Deryck.

'Didn't come, boss,' said the Captain, 'got sick day before we sailed, had to take Vish here instead,' nodding at the Tamil.

Deryck frowned, he'd check it out back on shore. He collected the passports, gave them to the Immigration fellers who were used to this shit, could spot a lifted photo at a hundred paces. You could see their eyes light up as they went to work.

Ten minutes later though and the senior Immigration feller comes over to Deryck, says, 'Looks like they check out.'

'You sure?' asked Deryck, feeling the raid decisively slip away from him.

The Immigration officer shrugged. 'I'm sure no one here's got a passport that's been fucked around with. Doesn't mean they're necessarily who the passport says they are. We'll interview them all anyway back at the office but as of now I'd have to say they look like they all check out.'

Deryck nodded, tried not to look like the world was falling in on him. 'OK,' he said, 'you take them over to the office. Let me know if anything, anything at all, comes up. Rest of us got more work to do on the boat.'

This was a lie but Deryck felt a little calmer once the crew had been led off to the Customs office. Deryck had Mr Omar show him and his guys around the boat, checking for stowaways, but he could just tell from the way Omar was behaving that he had nothing to hide.

They were just finishing a perfunctory search of the galley when Deryck's phone rang. 'Yes,' he said.

'McKenzie,' said McKenzie, 'how's it going down there?' his tone all matey.

Deryck could see him in his office checking his uniform was looking good, gearing up for the press conference. He swallowed hard.

'Nothing yet, sir,' he said, 'still searching the boat.'

'Hell do you mean?' said McKenzie, his voice changing instantly. 'Thought you told me you'd got their scam figured out. The Immigration officers: have they checked the passports yet?'

'Yes,' said Deryck, then, 'Look, let me just finish the search, I'll call you back in half an hour, sir, with a full update.'

'Better have some good news for me, son, we've shown a lot of faith in you over this.'

'Yes, sir, I know, sir,' said Deryck and clicked off, put the phone back in his pocket, a sense of utter dread coming over him, his dreams of promotion, of getting out of Butetown, speeding away from him.

He returned to the search with desperate energy but half an hour passed and there was no sign of anything but more and more crap furniture. The only thing that kept Deryck going was the expression on Captain Omar's face, something smug there, something that said he thought he was putting one over on Deryck. But whatever it was he was hiding, Deryck couldn't find it. He called the Immigration people. No luck there either. They were still interviewing, they said, but everyone was still checking out.

Deryck's mobile rang again. His first impulse was to ignore it, give himself a few more minutes before McKenzie chewed him out, sent him to direct traffic in Grangetown for the next five years. The phone kept on ringing. He closed his eyes momentarily then answered.

'Deryck?' It wasn't McKenzie, it was Lianna.

What the hell did she want? Worried that she couldn't see Val Dennison to shoot him?

'Yeah,' he said, 'what is it?'

'It's Val,' she said.

Deryck rolled his eyes. For Christ's sake.

'He's not here,' he said.

'No,' said Lianna sounding excited, not hysterical. 'I know he's not and I know where he is too.'

'Portugal?'

'Portugal? What are you talking about? He's on Steepholm – they dropped him off.'

Deryck's heart suddenly leaped up from the pit of his stomach. Steepholm was an island in the Bristol Channel, five miles or so from Cardiff. 'You sure?'

'Course I'm fucking sure. C'mon, Del, you've got a boat. Let's go.'

Deryck stood there on the deck, holding on to the

phone like it was the only thing anchoring him to the ground, thinking about it. Could it be true? Yes, well, he didn't see why not. He'd seen on the charts that you could land on Steepholm. Flatholm, its sister island, was easier but there were people on it all the time. Steepholm would be quieter. But if it was true, then what should he do? Not go there with a crazed woman with a gun, that was for sure. What he should do was get a police launch and do the job properly.

'Deryck, you there?' said Lianna's voice on the phone, but Deryck didn't answer, his attention instead caught by the arrival of another police car on the dockside. And the emergence from it of his boss, McKenzie. Even at this distance Deryck could see he wasn't happy.

'Look,' he said, picking up the phone again, 'are you really sure about this? How do you know?'

'I was in Spiller's office. Jerk thinks I fancy him, right, and I heard the phone call.'

'And you're sure he said Steepholm?' As Deryck was talking he could see McKenzie walking up the gang plank on to the boat. 'You're sure?'

'Yes,' said Lianna, 'Steepholm,' like she was talking to an imbecile, which, right at that moment, wasn't far off the mark.

He felt paralysed. McKenzie was coming on to the boat. Deryck deliberately ducked round towards the front of the boat, out of sight. 'Where are you?'

'By the Marina, of course. Waiting for you.'

Fuck, fuck, fuck, what to do? 'Look,' he said, 'just hang on, I'll call you back.'

He clicked the phone off, went round the bulkhead and slap into McKenzie.

'Well, Douglas,' said McKenzie – no Deryck now – 'you mind explaining this fuck-up to me?'

'They've got away,' said Deryck, feeling the sweat popping out on his forehead as he talked, hearing the pitiful unlikeliness of it. 'I think they may have left the boat already and taken a dinghy to Steepholm, sir. If you could let me have the launch I can check it out.'

McKenzie looked at him, laughed with no humour whatsoever. 'You're joking, son. After this fiasco, most you're going to be let loose with is the schools education pack. Now, why don't you run over to the Customs office tell the Immigration folk to stop wasting their time and I'll see you back in my office in half an hour.'

'Yes, sir,' said Deryck but McKenzie already had his back to him, hurrying off the boat back to his car, no doubt already planning the report that would blame everything on Deryck, no mention of the fact that it was McKenzie had the hard-on for Raj Impex in the first place.

His phone rang again.

'Yes?'

'You coming or what?' said Lianna.

'Yeah,' he said, 'I'm coming.' McKenzie could wait – this Steepholm thing turned out to be kosher then Deryck was a hero. If it was bollocks, then how much further in the shit could he be?

★　　★　　★

Fifteen minutes later Deryck was casting off, Lianna was sitting at the helm of the boat watching him, and he was filled with a heady mix of dread and excitement.

He'd kept on at Lianna for more information but she just said that was what she'd heard. Spiller had said, 'You're on Steepholm,' and then later, 'Stay there till dark.' She couldn't prove anything but she was going if she had to shag every last yachting twat in the club to get her there. That's what she'd said and Deryck believed her. So Steepholm it was.

Ten minutes and they were at the barrage. Deryck had phoned ahead on his mobile – no need for temperamental ship radios any more this close to land – to let them know they were approaching and they were able to head straight into the lock system. Lianna was visibly impatient as they waited for the water-levels to lower them gently down towards sea-level and Deryck suddenly wished he'd searched her before they got on the boat. He'd asked her if she'd got the gun and she'd laughed and said no need with you around is there but he should never have believed her. What really worried him was the thought that maybe he didn't care. This whole day was so far fucked up already.

Finally they were through the locks and the great barrage gates opened and they were out in the Channel. Looking back at the barrage, now they were through it, it was amazing how huge it was, rising a good sixty, seventy feet out of the sea. Made the dinghy feel tiny as Deryck headed out to sea, steering to the east of

Flatholm, peering through the gathering mist for a sign of Steepholm beyond.

In fact it wasn't till they'd almost completely rounded Flatholm, no easy task as the mist gave way to driving wind and rain, that the black hulk of Steepholm hove into view. At this distance it seemed to be just a sheer rock rising out of the sea. Deryck steadied the boat as best he could and picked up the chart. Looked like the only possible landing spot was a beach on the far side of the island facing the Somerset coast. Trouble was there were undersea rocks marked all over the place. Best bet seemed to be to stay close in to the island and pray.

As they got closer to the island Deryck could make out a building on the top of the cliffs, a squat grey structure, looked like a military building of some sort, and a glance down at the chart confirmed that it was a barracks. World War One, Two, or earlier he didn't know, and quickly stopped contemplating the question as the tidal current, combined with the wind, threatened to capsize them as he tried to make the turn around the eastern end of the island.

Five minutes of scrambled nerves later the boat was at last in calmer water and Lianna had stopped throwing up and Deryck had spotted the beach – just a break in the cliffs and a patch of rock and shingle but enough for a small boat to land on.

Again it was easier said than done and they both got soaked clambering off the dinghy and on to the beach. Deryck looked around for a welcoming committee: Val Dennison sat there with a gun, that kind of thing, but there was no one. One advantage of the bad weather, it had cloaked their arrival.

At beach-level there were a couple of ruined buildings: one was a Victorian pub, which seemed wildly out of place. There must have been a permanent barracks on the island at some point, he guessed. At the back of the beach there was a path cut into the cliff.

Deryck turned to Lianna, raised his eyebrows. 'What d'you reckon?'

Looking drenched and miserable, but still determined, she just nodded and said, 'Let's go.'

And so they started the trudge up the cliff path, thankfully a wide, well-made affair with the remnants of some kind of rail track embedded in it. Hard to imagine now, but obviously at some point this must have been part of the frontline of Britain's military fortifications, back when the main worry was the French approaching by sea.

As they climbed the weather became, if anything, worse. Presumably on a half-decent day they'd have had views across half Somerset, but today there was nothing but wind and rock and grey sea. Midway up the path they passed the ruins of a cottage and Deryck stiffened again, alert to any sign of life. There was none, but now, trudging up the remainder of the path, his brain started to clear, the adrenalin of getting to the island wearing off and replaced by the realisation that there were essentially two possibilities ahead. Either this was a fool's errand that would cost him his job, or else he was walking unarmed into who knew what danger. He checked his mobile. Surprise, surprise – no glimmer of a signal.

He pulled Lianna close to him, shouted in her ear to make himself heard over the wind and the cormorants, 'Look, we see anything, anything at all, we go back to the boat and we call and we wait. OK?'

'OK,' said Lianna, but the look on her face, the hunger there, made him wonder.

But what else was there to do? They were three-quarters of the way up a cliff; human nature kept him going all the way to the top. That and the sure knowledge that Lianna wasn't going to back down.

Finally they reached the top of the cliff path. Logic told Deryck that they had to be on the central plateau, though the mist was now such that you could barely see twenty yards ahead so it was hard to be sure. There was a choice of paths now – he followed the largest one, the one with the train tracks now clearly visible, and it soon led them to a big grey building, presumably the barracks they had seen from the sea.

Up close the building was in much better repair than any of the others down below. Up closer still, Deryck saw a sign saying 'Visitors' Centre'. There was no sign of any lights on. And surely no visitors ever showed up at this time of year. Was this the building Dennison was using?

As one, Deryck and Lianna flattened themselves against the wall of the barracks and started to inch round the outside looking for any sign that someone was inside. Ten minutes of this and Deryck was colder and wetter then he could remember being and all he could say was that if there were people inside they were being very discreet about it. All he could see through the few ground-level windows was a deserted hallway and a similarly deserted café area.

He pondered what to do next, Lianna looking at him like she expected him to have a plan. Fuck it, he thought then, the mist and rain could work for them as well as against them. Why not ring on the front door, then retire to the shadows and see what happened, whether there was any reaction from inside.

They tried it three times but if there was anyone inside they had nerves of steel and there was no response at all.

Finally Lianna turned to Deryck, said, 'Let's keep on going, see if there's some other place he could be.'

Unable to think of any better plan, Deryck nodded and they trudged on down the path further into the central plateau. They walked through nothing but rain and grass and the occasional concrete fortification for a while till Lianna pointed off to their right up an incline towards another squat grey building.

As they reached it, Deryck saw a sign saying 'Summit Battery'. At ground-level you could make out where the big guns must have been set up, pointing out to sea. And in one corner there were steps leading underground, to an ammunition store, most likely.

God only knew what would be down there these days. Rats, for sure. Deryck really, really, didn't want to go down there. Dark and underground and rat-infested, these were things he dreaded. He looked round at Lianna, sighed as he saw her heading straight for the steps.

Deryck was getting close to the end of his tether now.

Soaked and freezing and scared, no more than a shadow of the self-confident copper he'd been – what, only three hours ago. Walking down the steps into this underground bunker he felt like a kid again, scared and weak and only one unpredictable female to focus his trust on.

Thankfully there were only seven or eight steps down before Deryck felt himself at the bottom of the stairs. He could barely make out the shape of Lianna in front of him. Then he heard her strike a match and the place flared into light and it was just as he imagined, dark and empty apart from red eyes staring back at him.

He couldn't help it, he screamed and ran back up the steps and away from the battery. Went twenty yards before he caught himself and stood there taking great gulps of sea air till Lianna came up the stairs and rejoined him, put her arm around him.

'Don't like rats,' she said, the kindness he'd once heard in her voice returned.

'No,' he echoed, 'I don't like rats.'

They stood together there for a moment, surveying the island through the rain and the gathering gloom. No doubt there were other batteries, other potential storerooms out there, but Deryck wasn't about to find out. He just shook his head and Lianna looked at him and said, 'C'mon, let's get out of the rain,' and then they walked back to the barracks and this time Lianna walked straight up to the door and instead of knocking like they'd done before she just turned the handle and the door opened and they were inside.

Deryck savoured the luxury of not being rained on

and Lianna picked up a box of Dairy Milk from a counter and gave Deryck a bar and took another for herself and they ate the chocolate in silence.

Then Lianna said, 'C'mon, follow me,' and led Deryck into a back room where she turned the light on and there was a bed and fan heater which she switched on and they sat on the bed and warmed their hands in front of the fire and then Lianna took Deryck's warmed hands in hers and placed them round her neck and said, 'Do me now,' and wondering at how she knew him better than he knew himself he did her, took out all the anger and fear and frustration of the day on her, and only afterwards, the bruises already blooming on her, did he wonder if the whole thing, this whole crazy boat trip to Steepholm, had been no more than foreplay, that Lianna was this crazy, much crazier than his crazy mother, bitch who would take a man to a rat-infested island just for this.

And that's when it hit him. How utterly fucked he was. His job – the one thing that gave his life shape – now completely screwed. Would they sack him? Probably not – it's not easy to sack a copper. But it's easy enough to make their life unbearable – constant petty humiliations, the fast track replaced by the slow. And for why?

Because he'd done what the boss asked him to. Investigated Raj Impex. The unfairness of it made him want to cry out it's not my fault, like a kid. Without realising it he was burrowing into Lianna and she was holding him, stroking his head. As he became aware of it he almost rebelled. Wasn't it her fault too that he was here, that it had come to this, that the information he'd been given was all wrong? He'd placed his trust in a crazy woman. But she was holding him and whispering in his ear and he felt forgiveness flow through him. Felt it strong as love. He forgave her. He saw the bruises on her neck and he forgave himself. And kissed her there, around the neck, and she moved into him and kissed him and soon she offered him the rope and this time he shook his head and looked at her waiting for the familiar fire to come to her eyes, the demand for his violence, his anger, but it didn't come, she just laid her head back like a penitent, more a victim now than she ever was with a rope round her, the tears new to her eyes.

And then they heard the noise. Someone opening the front door of the barracks.

Deryck was out of bed in a second. He rolled on to the floor then, quietly as he could, he edged out of the door from the makeshift bedroom into the front café area. It was dark in there now, night having come down outside, and Deryck was trying to think where there might be something he could use as a weapon when the light came on and he found himself staring at a man with a gun.

'Who the fuck are you?' said the man, a well-built blond white man in his late thirties wearing a big black puffa jacket. 'Wild man of Steepholm?'

Deryck just stood there, stark naked, feeling more of a bloody idiot than he ever had in his life, but also in a weird way relieved. At least there was something going on here. He hadn't been chasing chimeras all the way. And somehow too being faced by a man with a gun wasn't as terrifying as he'd thought it would be – he'd never bucked up against a gun before, knives, yes, fists too many times, once a teenager with a crossbow, but never a gun before – and it was scary, sure, but it didn't paralyse him.

'You mind if I put some clothes on?' he said, pleased to hear his voice come out almost level.

'Be my guest,' said the man with the gun, keeping it trained on Deryck and following him into the back room, seemingly also just as calm as could be. Which changed pretty fast when he opened the door to the back room and saw Lianna standing there, pointing her own gun straight at him.

'Lee,' he cried out, 'what the fuck?' and for a moment his gun hand wavered, and Deryck took his chance in an instant, delivering a well-practised karate chop to the bloke's arm causing the gun to drop to the floor and the bloke to yelp with sudden pain.

Deryck swooped and picked up the bloke's gun, nodded to Lianna like they were a team, did this kind of thing all the time, and she held the gun on the feller – 'Don't move, Val,' she said, kind of confirming that the feller was indeed Val Dennison.

Deryck dressed himself and held Val's gun on Val while Lianna did likewise, Val's eyes opening wide when he saw the bruises on Lianna's neck but keeping his mouth shut, biding his time, thought Deryck, and sure enough, once they had all moved into the front room it was Val who started talking, his attention entirely focused on Lianna.

'Knew it was a bad idea taking you here, Lee,' he said. 'Might have guessed you'd figure it out.'

Lianna just stared at him, like she was willing him to wind her up, give her the jumpstart to pull the trigger.

Deryck jumped in to break the silence. 'You've been here before?' he said.

Lianna didn't reply, Dennison did.

'Yeah,' he said, 'didn't she tell you? Came here for the weekend, we did, before, before . . .' He stopped, his eyes widening, seeing the fury in Lianna's eyes. 'Oh,' he said, and now for the first time he actually looked frightened, 'that's what this is about, is it? You blaming me, now, are you?'

Deryck stared at Dennison then Lianna, trying to work out what the hell was going on. Had Lianna had an affair with Dennison – was that it?

Then, at last, Lianna spoke, her voice low and guttural. 'She was your wife.'

'She was your sister, Lee. Beam in your own eye, don't you think?'

Lianna flinched, like she'd been slapped. Her hand tensed on the trigger then relaxed as she shouted back, 'You fucking bastard, you killed her, I should fucking shoot you now.'

Even as she said the words though, Deryck could feel the tension ebb a little. Like maybe that was the moment of truth and instead of shooting she'd shouted. All depended on what Dennison said next.

'She's gone, Lee, I'm not proud, you're not proud, but it's over, Jule's dead. She drowned and maybe it was because I was a bastard to her, maybe because she found out about you and me, or maybe just maybe it was a bloody accident. Only thing that's certain is she's gone. You can shoot me, you can beat yourself up, or get your boyfriend here to do it, won't change anything.'

Christ, thought Deryck, guy was certainly cool under pressure, might even have a point about Lianna and her appetite for pain, but he'd worry about that later. For the moment the only priority was how to dismantle this situation.

Once again Dennison was ahead of him. 'Look,' he said, his attention still entirely focused on Lianna, like Deryck wasn't even there, 'you're not going to shoot me. If you were, you would have done it by now. Trouble is, you know you're as much to blame as I am,' and even as he spoke he was standing up and walking towards her and she was pointing the gun in his face and Deryck was thinking he should do something, but what?

If he used his gun he was as likely to kill one as the other, and then the moment had gone anyway as Dennison reached out his hand for Lianna's gun and then there was a bang and Deryck threw himself to the floor and there was shouting and then everyone stood up and no one was visibly hurt and Dennison had a gun and Deryck had a gun and Lianna was shouting and kicking Dennison on the legs and Dennison belted her across the face and stepped back and yelled, 'Shut the fuck up,' and then there was quiet.

And again it was Dennison who took control of the situation, turning his attention for the first time to Deryck.

'OK,' he said, 'you've got a gun. I've got a gun. She doesn't have a gun. Probably I could threaten to shoot her and make you give me your gun but can we please not do any of that shit? OK with you if we just work out a way we can all leave this island, way we got here? Which I'm assuming is by boat. You a sailor?'

'Yes,' said Deryck, his tongue feeling rusty in his mouth.

'Good man,' said Dennison, 'and are you just her lucky boyfriend, or you got some other interest in this business?' He stared at Deryck, his mind clearly working overtime, then smiled broadly. 'Got it. You're the copper, aren't you? The scapegoat?'

Deryck stared at him. 'You mind letting me in on what's so funny?'

'Sure,' said Dennison looking down quickly at his watch. 'Approximately an hour from now there will be a boat landing on the beach, nice little motor launch come to pick up the cargo, and you know who'll be on it?'

Deryck stared at him, not wanting to say the name that was coming unbidden to his mind. Waited for Dennison to say it, which he did with evident relish.

'McKenzie. Your boss. Done you up like the proverbial, hasn't he, old son?'

Deryck stared at him, tried it out for size in his mind, fitted all too well. Jesus, hadn't his father as much as told him so that morning? Christ, that morning was all it was, felt like a lifetime been and gone since then. He'd been given the rope and he'd obligingly hung himself. And it was neat enough, wasn't it? New boy comes in, gets over-enthusiastic, leads team on a wild-goose chase, meanwhile the illegals get smuggled in through the back door. Talking of which.

'So where are they, the illegals?' he said. 'You left them outside in the rain?'

Dennison's smile widened, led into a full-blown laugh. 'Illegals! You seriously believed that shit? You think it's worth smuggling two, three people at a time? Fifty in a container, maybe, but all that swapping the crew over shit would be way too expensive, 'less you were expecting Osama himself on board.'

He raised his eyebrows, clearly seeing something in Deryck's face. 'Oh, maybe you were. No, Del boy, you don't smuggle people from Georgia, you smuggle pure Afghan smack. Tons of it around since the Americans liberated the place. Just waiting for a friendly local import—export firm to lend a helping hand. And a friendly copper looking for an early retirement on the Costa.

'So how d'you want to play this, feller? You going to go death or glory on me? Take on the odds of shooting me before I can shoot you or the lovely Lianna here, and then, even if you come through that, have to take your chances with McKenzie and his boys, or d'you want to make a deal?'

Deryck tried to think rationally about it. Half of him just felt like blasting away with the gun in his hand. Kill

Dennison. Kill Lianna. Kill himself too. He let his eyes leave Dennison for a moment, seeking Lianna, but she was just huddled on the floor, whispering to herself and he felt the stirrings of an emotion he'd rarely felt and treated with contempt when he did. He felt pity for her and sensed too that pity was not something to be ashamed of, did not have to demean both pitier and pitied, but could be close to love. In that moment of pitying her he found himself with an imperative. He would protect her. He would save her the way no one but God saved his mum. He would do the right thing. He would go along with Dennison's plan.

'Yeah,' he said, 'I want to make a deal.'

Dennison smiled like he'd never for a moment thought there was any other possible outcome. 'Good,' he said. 'You've got a boat, yeah?'

'Yeah,' said Deryck, 'down at the beach.'

'Well then,' said Dennison, 'we'd better get moving before your boss shows up.'

A frantic two hours later they were within sight of Llantwit Major Beach: Deryck, Dennison and a still near-comatose Lianna, plus a boatload of Afghan smack. First they'd scuttled Dennison's own boat, the dinghy he'd used to get from the *Feroza* to the island, the idea being that maybe McKenzie would figure that Val and his cargo were lost at sea. Then they'd loaded the heroin on to Deryck's boat and set course for the nearest quiet beach, which had meant a tricky sail around Flatholm and past Barry Dock. And now Deryck was ostentatiously looking at his charts, checking whether the tide would let them into Llantwit, using the time to take stock of what was going on.

The deal had been simple – Dennison had given Deryck his little black book full of times, dates and bank-account details – enough to send McKenzie to prison for decades. In exchange, Deryck was giving Dennison the chance to escape with the best part of a million pounds worth of heroin.

Did he trust Dennison to stick to the deal once they made the shore? Not really, he half expected Dennison to try to kill them both. What he was going to do about it, he wasn't sure. He still had a gun and he felt like he could probably take care of himself, but Lianna, Lianna was the problem. Ever since she'd seen Dennison and he'd confronted her with her part in her sister's death she'd been practically comatose. Even now she was just huddled on the bottom of the boat.

Except, he noticed, she wasn't. She was standing up and she had something in her hand. Oh Christ, she had his flare gun and she was pointing it not up at the sky but straight at the petrol tank and now Dennison had seen her too and was shouting and diving towards her but too late.

She fired the flare and there was an eye-searing flash and a bang and a smell and then there was burning, the petrol tank exploding into flame, and in seconds the boat was an inferno and Deryck reacted with pure instinct, grabbed Lianna by one hand and just threw her into the water and then dived off himself and as he surfaced, kicking his shoes off in the freezing water, he looked back and saw Dennison still on board, surrounded by fire, desperately trying to rescue his narcotic fortune, and then there was no boat, just flame on the water and no sign of Dennison, and nothing for Deryck to do except turn and hold on to Lianna and pray he had the strength to swim to shore pulling her dead weight.

Only she wasn't a dead weight, the cold of the water seemed to have shocked her back into life, and she shook his hand away and started swimming hard for the land and thank Christ the tide was with them and in minutes successive waves had deposited first Lianna then Deryck on the beach and Deryck lay there for a moment feeling the wonder of continued life and hearing Lianna's long retching breaths alongside him.

And then he summoned the energy to stretch his hand towards her and she must have had the same impulse at the same instant because he sensed her fingers reaching out to clasp his, her white hand in his black hand, and as they touched, he let himself hope that maybe this was their second chance.

ACKNOWLEDGEMENTS

Thanks first of all to Phil John for all his input into *Temperance Town*. Thanks to Su West at the *Big Issue Cymru* for commissioning half a dozen of the stories that have made their way into this book. Thanks to Richard Thomas for commissioning 'Tiger Princess'. Thanks to my agent Abner Stein and my editor Mike Jones. Thanks also to Colin Midson and to Rosemarie Buckman for all their work on my behalf. Thanks always to Charlotte.

A NOTE ON THE AUTHOR

John Williams is the author of two books of non-fiction, one concerned with American crime fiction, the other with a murder and its hinterland, and five books of fiction, of which four, including this one, are set in his home town of Cardiff, where he lives with his family.

A NOTE ON THE TYPE

The text of this book is set in Bembo. This type was first used in 1495 by the Venetian printer Aldus Manutius for Cardinal Bembo's *De Aetna*, and was cut for Manutius by Francesco Griffo. It was one of the types used by Claude Garamond (1480–1561) as a model for his Romain de L'Université, and so it was the forerunner of what became standard European type for the following two centuries. Its modern form follows the original types and was designed for Monotype in 1929.